JULIAN

STEELE RIDERS MC 2ND GENERATION
BOOK 2

C.M. STEELE

THE STEELE PRESS

Julian Martinez has lived his life with one goal — to become the best doctor he can be. Discipline, focus, and sacrifice have always been his guiding principles. Nothing could shake his resolve... until Everly, his best friend's little sister, walked into his life and turned his world upside down.

She's become his quiet obsession, the one temptation he's sworn to resist. But when unexpected circumstances make Everly his new roommate for the next several months, Julian's iron control begins to crack. Every shared glance, every accidental touch, every late-night conversation chips away at the walls he's built. And when temptation sleeps just a few feet away, even the most disciplined man can only hold out for so long.

Everly has known of Julian for years, but meeting him in person changed everything. He's older, accomplished, and seemingly untouchable, yet she can't ignore the pull between them. Now, fate has placed her right where she wants to be, in his home, in his space, and hopefully, in his heart. She's determined to prove that age, distance, and circumstance mean nothing when two people are meant to be together.

The question is... how long can Julian resist before desire wins?

CHAPTER ONE

JULIAN

I'M MONITORING TWO PATIENTS WHILE READING UP ON THEIR conditions. Since I've just finished the fourth year of my residency, there is still a great deal for me to learn. I've been so invested in my books that I take a bite of my lunch, and I spit it back out. "Shit." It's ice-cold and now ruined.

Frustrated, I toss it in the trash and snag a cup of black coffee from the remaining pot on the counter. I don't know how long it's been there, but I need something, and I don't have long before I'm summoned back to work. Being a resident isn't an easy thing, but I've always wanted to be a doctor, and nothing will stop me. Nothing. Not even my other obsession.

My stomach rumbles, but a meal will have to wait until my shift ends in a few hours.

The door to the break area opens, and my best friend—soon-to-be former roommate, Drake—enters. I lift my head from my readings. "Hey, how about you come over for dinner tonight at five?" Drake asks.

"Come over? We live together," I remind him. Since his residency programs recently ended, he's selected where he'll practice and has been offered a job.

My program ends next year, and I've already got my mind and heart made up because it's been ingrained in me since I was a kid. There is a position waiting for me at Steeleville Medical Center alongside my mother and Dr. Joseph Simmons, who is one of my Steele Rider "uncles," as I like to call them, or, as everyone else calls him, Doc.

"No. My mother is throwing a last-minute dinner to celebrate the end of my program and my departure to Seattle." He's taken a Family Medicine position in Seattle that pays well and gets him far away from Texas.

"At your mother's?"

"Yes."

Dinner at his mother's automatically means that I'll see Drake's sister. God, his little sister. My dick hardens at just the simple mention of her name—Everly.

She's twenty now. A lot older than when I first met the little temptation. Four years ago, she was a petite girl with long brown hair and light brown doe eyes that captivated me when I was in the middle of my graduation speech.

There were no words for the way my heart leaped out of my chest. Somehow, I spotted her through the masses, and my gaze was laser-focused on her the entire time. She was too tiny for me to see anything besides her perfect face, but it was unmistakable that she had a profound effect on me, and when I finally barreled through that crowd, I found her in the arms of my best friend.

"Julian, Earth to Julian." Drake waves his hand in my face. "Whoa, where the fuck did you go?"

"Sorry. I've been thinking about these patients," I lie, taking a quick glance at my books and then back at Drake.

He scoffs and shakes his head. "Yeah, that's just like you. I'm so glad my practice is going to be laid back and I won't be spending much time at the hospital—unlike you. So, what do you say? Are you coming, or are you going to hurt my mom's feelings?"

"I'm supposed to be back here by ten for a second round."

"Really?"

"Yeah, to cover an overflow."

"You can still come by. It's clear you haven't eaten, and my mom's going to be upset if you don't."

What a prick. "You know my parents raised me better than that." His father died a long time ago, so their mom is everything to them. "I'll be there."

My stomach turns at the idea of how I'll react when I see Everly again. It has been at least two months since our last confrontation, and when I say confrontation, I mean it. She was pissed because I told her the outfit she was wearing wasn't appropriate for the party we were attending, and her mother and brother agreed with me and made her change.

Normally, it would have been fine if she wasn't my fucking obsession, but the idea of anyone else ogling her makes me violent, something I normally am not. Still, she was furious, calling me all kinds of names and telling me I wasn't her brother or her daddy.

I got the strangest arousal when she called me Daddy. Maybe it was the way she sassed the fuck out of me. There was no way I wanted to be her brother, but damn, I got turned on every single time she gave me any attitude. It made my hand itch, and I wanted to bend her over and paddle her ass.

"That's great. I'll text my mom and let her know that you're coming. She'll be so excited to see you. I've got to go and finish packing up my shit. You know I'm scheduled to leave next week."

"Yeah. I'm actually going to miss your stupid-ass remarks and late-night escapades."

"No, you're not. Don't lie. You'll be glad the house will have fewer female visitors."

"Yes, especially the nurses." Drake brings a woman home almost every damn day off. I'd come home to some random chick in my kitchen at least once a week. I was surprised to see the same girl more than once.

All I ask is that they come out of the room clothed. He'd shrug like it's no big deal, but I have to see these women and it's not acceptable. Since then, I have also come out of my bedroom fully clothed.

"You'll go to your siblings a little bit more for actual company because we know you won't bring any women home."

"True, although my siblings are as busy as I am."

"A bunch of nerds," he teases. I have four siblings: three brothers and one sister. It's a lot, but my parents are happy that the house is always crazy loud and busy. My parents quit making babies to focus on their careers and raising us. A houseful of small children was more than enough while still managing their work.

"That's the truth. My brother Rick is a cop, working alongside my father right now. He wants to be a detective, which scares my mother, of course."

"Well, tell him not to do undercover work and he'll be safer."

"That's what I say. Besides, he's a tough fucker," I add. We've all taken training classes. There isn't a Steele Rider male who hasn't been well trained to fight. After the years of gangs and drugs that came passing through town, our fathers made sure we could handle ourselves and protect our families. I'll forever be grateful. I may be a doctor, but I'll do anything to keep those I love safe.

Love. My thoughts immediately go to Everly. She doesn't know it, but my heart has always been hers. It's a tough struggle, and I can't even express how I've tied myself into knots trying to fight the attraction while looking my best friend in the eye and telling him that I'm just not into dating. No—I want only one woman, and if I could, I'd have her screaming my name through the entire apartment, but he'd fucking kill me.

Drake double taps the table with his knuckles and then stands. "I'll see you later."

"See ya." He leaves and I attempt to focus on the books in front of me, but my mind has lost all thoughts of medical care. Images of Everly in my arms as she begs me to fill her up flood my brain. It's wrong as fuck because she's twenty and I'm turning thirty in a few weeks. She probably thinks I'm a creepy old man.

The last time I saw her, she'd changed her hair color, adding blonde highlights throughout, making her appear more mature. She's in a Cosmetology program, and it's almost over. She and her classmates had worked on her hair. It came out perfect. Everly looked sexy already, but this added a little extra sass to the bratty girl I knew. I wanted to grab her hair, pull her to me, and shut her up with my mouth.

I wonder what she'll look like tonight. The thoughts consume me, and it makes the rest of my shift too long.

I climb in my truck and head to our apartment, which isn't too far from Dallas General, to shower and freshen up. It's about thirty minutes later when I jump on my motorcycle and ride over to the Mitchells' residence in Arlington. Normally I'd drive after a long shift, but since I have to rush back and forth, I prefer my bike.

Shit. I hope Everly doesn't cause me to do something stupid, like kiss her in front of her family.

When I arrive, I'm greeted by Mrs. Mitchell. "Please come in, Julian."

She kisses my cheek, and I give her a polite hug. She's a nice woman who has always been sweet to me. "Thank you, Mrs. Mitchell."

"How many times must I ask you to call me Carol?"

"Sorry, Carol. You're looking lovely tonight."

"Don't hit on my mother. She's got a special surprise waiting in the other room that won't take kindly to it," Drake says.

"Whoa, replacing me," I tease, pressing my hand to my chest.

She pats my cheek, looking almost sad, as if she isn't hiding a grin. "Sorry. You're too young for me."

"Don't make me kick your ass," Drake growls.

"Like you could. Besides, you know damn well I'd never hit on your family, you asshole." I shake my head and walk forward, nearly colliding with Everly, who is walking and talking on her phone. I throw my arms out and catch her before we slam into each other.

"Sorry. I wasn't paying attention," she stammers out.

"Obviously not," I grumble, staring at the cell phone in her hands. Who the fuck is she talking to that had all of her attention? Irrationally, I want to crush that damn thing and never let her make a call again. She's an adult and not my property, but it doesn't change the way she gets under my skin every time we meet.

She glares at me, huffing with her nostrils flaring and her pretty, light brown eyes staring daggers at me. "You don't have to be a jerk about it. You're built like a brick wall. You'll survive. I'm the one who was steamrolled by a giant."

"Still, all the more reason to be careful, little girl. You don't want to end up on your back." The thought of her on her back with her legs on my shoulders or wrapped around my waist as she takes every inch of me fills my head, and I want to slam my fist into a wall. I've fought this attraction for years for good reason.

"Are you giving him shit again?" Drake says, stepping in the way to create a divide.

"He's just barking at me for accidentally bumping into him. I'm going to school. I'll be back later," she says, pushing past me as if I'm nothing but a nuisance.

"You're not staying for dinner?" I ask, watching her backside like a damn meal itself. *Damn it, Martinez, get a hold of yourself.*

"No. I have a class, and Mom forgot. Must be the new guy. Well, I'll see you all later—or *not*."

"What's that supposed to mean?" I question. She's old enough to move out and everything, but is she not planning on coming home tonight? Who the fuck is she going to be with? That motherfucker must have a death wish. Drake told me she's single and doesn't date.

"I mean, you two will be going home by the time I get back. Isn't that the modus operandi?" she huffs, scowling at me.

"Sorry, we're busy trying to become doctors, little brat."

"Sorry we all can't be saving the world. Some of us are trying to keep people from aging poorly." She reaches up and brushes the sides of my hair where a hint of gray has appeared. I started seeing the gray about six months ago. My father says it runs in his side of the family down the line, and many in their early twenties were prematurely gray. At least I made it to twenty-nine before it happened, and I'm not going bald. I had classmates that were bald at twenty-three.

"Be careful, little problem child. Do you plan on putting on a jacket? It's not summer yet." It isn't freezing out, but there's a chill in the air now that it's later in the evening. Soon it'll be hot all the time, but it's about sixty-five.

"I'm not a child anymore. I just turned twenty. It's not my fault you're an old man, and my hoodie is by the door, Daddy. Don't get bent out of shape. I'm not going to catch a cold." She keeps fucking with me. She's the one who is going to get bent...bent over.

"I need a word with you, Ev," Drake growls, walking his sister right past me and toward the door.

"Come on. I'd like you to meet my betrothed," Mrs. Mitchell says, taking me away from the woman who gets my dick hard and my heart pounding. I walk away reluctantly, but she's wrong because I'm going to be here when she gets home. This conversation isn't over with. Maybe it's time that I start acting my age.

"Fiancé?" I question.

"Yes."

Mrs. Mitchel lost her husband about ten years ago, but I didn't even know she was seeing anyone seriously. Her take on relationships isn't like mine. I plan on waiting until I finish residency because I have a goal in mind, and women are a distraction.

Drake gets his dating habits from his mother. The revolving door is something Mrs. Mitchell has perfected with her men. She admits that no one compares to the man she lost, so she'll never marry again. I'm actually shocked.

"Yes. Drake hasn't told you?" she asks, scowling at her son, who's behind me.

"No."

"Well, I suppose it is new." She introduces me to this dweeb-looking fuck named Harold. He's polite, but I don't give a fuck because as much as I was afraid of seeing Everly tonight, I'm pissed that she's not here.

Throughout dinner, we all make small talk, and then we get to the main reason I was invited for the evening.

"So, Drake is leaving in one week and as it happens, we are leaving in two weeks." My fork freezes mid-bite.

"You and Everly are moving?" I question, feeling my heart is about to explode with that news. I've taken for granted that she'll always be around. It never occurred to me that the little glimpses of Everly that I've had over the years would be stolen from me in one way or another. The idea is foolish, short-sighted, and egotistical. I could kick myself.

"No, Everly still has four months of school left in her Cosmetology program, so she can't go, but Harold lives in Florida, and I'm moving with him." My head tilts to the side as I consider the ramifications. Everly will be here in Arlington all alone.

"So, what's going to happen to Everly? She's going to keep the house?"

"No. I've already listed the house, and she's not working at the moment." Drake told me she has a job at the local restaurant by their house. I came in once and, of course, it happened to be the only day she wasn't working. A week later, she was let go due to her calling off. Drake told me it was because of her best friend. He doesn't like her.

"Is she getting an apartment or something closer to her school?" I ask, wondering if the school actually has a dorm.

"No, there's nothing available that she can afford. Besides, we don't think it's safe for her to be a single young female living alone." I nod. Neither do I.

Drake scoots his chair in and then steeples his fingers. "Here's the thing, buddy. Since I'm moving out, I was thinking that she can take over my room." My mouth falls open, but I quickly shut it and attempt to keep a neutral expression.

He puts his hand up to stop my protests. "It's not like you party like I do and, well, you don't need the money…but I can still pay my half of the rent." My parents own the apartment building, so that's not the issue, but I can't believe what I'm hearing. Does he have any sense in his head? Can he not sense the lust I feel for her?

"What do you mean? You want Everly to move in with me?" I ask them.

"Yeah—who better to take care of her and keep her safe while she finishes school?" Keep her safe. That is the furthest thing from my mind when it comes to certain parts of her body. They aren't going to be protected from me.

"We're going to make some coffee," Mrs. Mitchell says, taking her man with her so Drake and I can talk.

"Um…I'm not sure it's a good idea. It's not like I'm home at all. She'll practically be living by herself," I say, hoping to dissuade my best friend from pestering me, but he just smiles at me, and I'm certain that I've only strengthened my case.

As the words leave my lips, my mind wanders to the day I met the young woman. She was already a torturous little thing, like now. I had tried to maintain a straight face as the words left my mouth so no one would be any the wiser about the effect she had on me. Only then, I was standing in front of a crowd of three hundred graduates, my parents, her mom, and, most importantly, my best friend, when I first spotted the most delectable beauty in front of me.

"That's even better. She won't be a pain in the ass then. I know my little sister annoys the shit out of you, Jules," he teases, using the nickname she calls me. It doesn't annoy me; it gets me rock fucking hard. Everything she does gets me stiff, and it's become a distraction I don't need. For over four years, I've been able to keep our meetings to a minimum and avoid her at all costs, even though I've missed her and hope I won't ruin a chance at a future.

"So, you decided to ask me for a favor while, in fact, annoying me as well?"

"It's not like that. It's only temporary. She's finishing her Cosmetology program and then getting a gig in Steeleville, thanks to the connections with your mom." My mom? What the hell is my mom doing with Everly's career?

"Besides, I'm starting my new job in Seattle, so it's not like I can have her with me." He sighs.

Damn. Well, I know why he doesn't want his little sister tagging along with him. He's a fuck boy and a half. My best friend had a girl on each arm in college for all four years, and it hasn't changed. If she's following him around, he can't have fun.

"Oh my God, just tell him the truth. You don't want me cramping your style, and you said he doesn't like pussy so I shouldn't be a problem." My temptress storms into her mom's dining room in nothing but a pair of tiny shorts and a tank top that should be fucking banned. That's not what she was wearing when she left. Her hair is different, and she has on makeup. A pang of jealousy rumbles in my chest. I check my watch, and it's eight, so she was only gone for three and a half hours. It's also a reminder that I need to leave.

"Now, that's not true, Julian." Drake tries to defend himself, but I know better. I just flip him off because I'm never bothered by his shit talking. Hell, that's one of the reasons we're friends. We dig into each other, and we don't get offended.

"Don't lie to him," Everly huffs, trying to protect me like the sweet girl she is. I don't miss the tough expression in her eyes.

"Do you want to go with Mom and Harold?" he challenges her.

"No." The resignation in her voice irritates me because she's actually hurt by it.

"Well, then, shut the fuck up." I almost snap on him, but then I remember that I'm supposed to hate the damn little brat.

"Look, I hate to break up this little sibling squabble, but I've got to be at the hospital in two hours for my next shift, and you are both giving me a damn headache. If you're not going to be a pain in my ass, then it will be fine if you move in."

"Yay! Thank you," she squeals and throws her arms around me, giving me a giant hug with her massive tits pressing against my chest. Damn, she smells incredible, and I steal a brief sniff. Fuck. I'm instantly solid and unsure how to react. I don't put my arms around her, and I definitely keep my face away from hers because I'll slam her lips to mine.

"Come on, Ev. Give the man some breathing room," Carol says, coming into the room with a tray of coffee.

"Sorry. She can be a bit much, and that's why she needs someone to watch after her—always sweet and naïve. Julian isn't going to let any asshole pricks take advantage of you. He'll keep you safe from all those guys trying to score."

"Whatever. I'm not a little girl." I could feel it.

"You would think so, but you haven't had a serious boyfriend." Immediately, I'm heated and ready to bust heads. The idea of any fucks lurking around her makes my blood boil.

"You can have the spare bedroom, and you have to be tidy —unlike this asshole." I'm not finished, because there's one rule I won't let slide. "And, little girl, no fucking boys in my house." It's a hard and fast rule that won't be violated unless a fucker wants his bones broken.

She gasps as if that's a deal breaker, but I'm sure that's the reason they want her little ass in my watchful gaze. Which is fucking stupid of them because I'm the worst person to be put in charge of her purity protection. I'm like a damn wolf in charge of the chicken coop. "That's fine," she huffs, turning on her heel and sending her long, perfectly coiffed ponytail swinging back and forth like a pendulum. And I want it wrapped in my fist.

As soon as I leave, my hand is on my cell phone. "Uncle Cyber, I need a favor. I need cameras installed in my place in ten days. I'm going to have a guest staying, and I need the place extra secured."

"Secured or protected?" he questions.

"Both." I want men to be able to look over my property on occasion when necessary.

"Okay. How many rooms? Exterior, or just interior?"

"Both, and I'm going to need a few little extras," I add. By the time I'm at the hospital for work, I feel an ounce better about my future roommate, but then I see my mother approaching. "Dr. Martinez, good evening," she says.

"Good evening, Mother." I know she gets a thrill out of calling me *Doctor,* and I love it too. "Are you done with your shift?"

"Just some administrative paperwork and then your father is picking me up for a late-night dinner at the steakhouse. Do you want us to bring you something to eat?" she asks. That sounds delicious right now. I rub my stomach and nod.

"That sounds good. I'll be working overnight, and I was in a bit of a rush and didn't pack another meal. I rode my motorcycle into work today after I stopped by the Mitchells' for dinner, but you know I could eat more," I confess. With my build, I burn an excessive amount of calories, and the only meal I managed to scarf down today was the one Mrs. Mitchell made.

Her brow cocks up, and she dips her head with her lips curled. "Oh, really? How did that go?"

"From the look on your face, you probably already know." Like my body and brain are fighting an all-out war.

"Well, considering you're obsessed with little Everly, I'm sure it's never easy leaving without her over your shoulder like a damn caveman." She pats my cheek.

"She's my best friend's little sister, and they've just made that shit way worse."

"What happened?"

"They've asked me to watch after her, letting her move in

with me for at least four months until she finishes school and then gets a gig."

"Are you serious?" she says as she begins to grin and bounces on her heels like she's a teen again. If my father saw her right now, I'm sure she'd be over his shoulder and carried into the nearest unoccupied room. Those two are bad, even in their older ages. They love the idea of love so much that it makes it hard not to share their sentiment. Maybe it's why I've waited for the right girl, and why I've never given up on the idea that maybe one day Everly and I will be right for each other.

"Why? Are you happy?"

"She's twenty now, and you'll have her feet away from you. What are you waiting for?"

"It's not that simple. Have you forgotten that I'm nearly a decade older, and that Drake wants me to keep men away from her, not fuck his innocent little sister?"

"Yes, I suppose you have a point there, but I guess you need to decide what's more important to you: your happiness, or his. You'll have time to decide, and you have patients that need your attention." She slaps my chest with a stack of patient records. "Get to it, Dr. Martinez."

I roll my eyes and grumble, "Yes, Mother." She leaves me, and then I'm met with Nurse Matteson for a run-through. We're about to get started when we're called in for a GSW —a gunshot wound to the chest. This is going to be a long night.

I work through my twelve-hour shift without allowing Everly to cloud my thoughts. It's one of the good things about being an Emergency Medicine doctor in a major city like Dallas. There is always something keeping you on your toes, especially on a Friday night. Still, the second I get on my motorcycle, Everly is in my head again.

After my shift is over, I drive to my parents' house. They are sitting on the porch drinking some tea and smiling at me when I get to the steps.

"Sweetheart, what's wrong? Are you tired?" she asks, pulling out of my father's relaxed embrace. Exhausted, actually.

"Nothing, Mother." I raise my hand up to stop her from rushing to my side. I love her concern, but I'm fine.

"Don't bullshit us, son. Is this about what your mother mentioned to me earlier?" I should have known that she would tell him. They have no secrets. It's midday on Saturday, and the Texas sun is blazing down on me. The warmth doesn't help my fatigue.

I sigh and rub my hand over my stubble. "Of course. There's not much I can do."

My father stands up and meets me at the bottom of the steps, pressing his hand on my shoulder. "There's a lot you can do, but I bet you're full of tension and pent-up energy for her." He raises his brows with a knowing look. He knows I'm suffering sexually.

I want her beyond belief. At my age, I should be getting pussy regularly, but that isn't the case. My parents don't know the truth, but he knows at the very least I've been waiting for Everly, which is stupid since I'm not even sure she's a virgin. As much as I'm obsessed, I haven't kept track, and Drake has implied she's had some boyfriends.

"Come on, sweetheart. We'll make you some food."

"No, I should probably go home and get ready. There's a lot to do in the house before she comes to stay next week."

"Next week? So soon?"

"Yes, that's what Drake said before I left after reminding me not to have anyone touch his sister."

"And you suppose that anyone includes you as well?"

"Of course it does. Is there a brother out there who would throw his sister at his friends?"

"No, but son, you're a hell of a catch. If there was a friend that a man was going to send his sister to, it would definitely be you."

"Thanks, Dad. I'll see you guys later. I just stopped by to say hello."

"Take care, and let me know if you need any help to get the room ready."

"I will probably have a lot of work this week, but I'm sure you're busy as well."

"Actually, I have the next couple of days off. So, if you need me, I'm all yours."

"I'll make a list tonight because I work tomorrow."

CHAPTER TWO

EVERLY

I take a calming breath the second I close my bedroom door knowing that Julian said yes. I'm going to be staying with Julian for four months. I'm hoping that's enough time to convince him that we belong together, and that my insane crush isn't one-sided. My mom swears Julian is hiding his feelings like a young schoolboy, and that's why he perpetually avoids me. For nearly four years, he never knew I existed.

Unfortunately, due to his schedule, we never got a chance to meet until that fateful day at graduation, when I swear he barreled down from the stage, knocking over strangers just to get to us, and that's when he stopped in his tracks, seeing my brother hug me. He frowned, and I pulled my head away from my brother's shoulder.

Drake turned around and shouted, "Hey, Julian! Your speech was epic. Not that I expected anything different." He pulled him into an embrace, bringing Julian inches from me. Those gorgeous blue eyes met mine, and I could feel my chest burst with excitement. All the boys that had caught my attention quickly faded into the background. Nothing compared. I'd never had a real boyfriend, and the only kiss I'd had happened the day before graduation. I swore after that the only man I wanted to kiss me was Dr. Julian Martinez.

Our eyes met, and I swear my heart stopped beating for a whole five seconds until my mom pinched my arm. "Everly, this is your brother's best friend, Julian. It's about time you two finally meet."

My brother released his grip, and I lost any common sense. "Oh, my goodness, congratulations." I quickly threw my arms around him and gave him a big squeeze. My breasts touched his broad chest, and I could hear him groan. "Whoa, whoa, whoa, little sis. Leave the man alone. You're still in high school. He's a little too old for you. Sorry she's in *'the chasing boys'* stage." That was a big damn lie. The boys chased me, and I sent them on their way. Unfortunately, some could be persistent, but so was a taser.

He let out a little growl. "Chasing boys? Aren't you only sixteen?" he questioned, as if I was too young to be interested in boys.

"Yes. And my brother's an idiot."

"Well, I've gotta go. My parents are waiting for me.

Congratulations, Drake." They shook hands and then parted ways.

"I'll see you later, buddy." Julian walked away from me without another word.

From that day on, I had the biggest crush and the ultimate goal of getting Julian Martinez to marry me. It's insane because he's ten years older than me and a doctor, but my heart and soul belong to that damn sexy man. Now is my chance to claim him, but I've only got four months to make it happen.

I have to pack everything in my bedroom. The rest of the house will be moved into storage, but I'm not sure if I'm keeping everything. Between school and time, I need to start immediately.

What would be acceptable to take to his place? I swear I've thought of this a thousand times over the last couple of years, but seriously, he is the man of my dreams, so what do you actually take with you? Would he find my stuffed animals too childish? My entire bedroom is shades of pink, and I love the color. Would he be annoyed and turned off by the girly things? Do we have to share a bathroom?

I was never allowed in their apartment, so I don't know how big it is. What if it's a box? My brother used to bring girls there, so it's big enough for that. Or did Julian get a show every damn time? Did he watch? Or worse…did he share them? I try to wash that thought and the subsequent image from my head and focus on the move. I'll have to check with my brother. I hope to hell it's not gross. Maybe

I'll go in there early and scrub it down. I hope we're taking my bed there. It's a smaller bed than my brother's, but I don't want his scummy, nut-stained bed. Disgusting.

My mom probably doesn't have the extra money to pay for movers, so I'm not sure how all my things are getting there. I wonder if Harold will be helping to foot the bill. My brother might be a doctor, but he's not at a doctor's pay just yet, and I'm sure it's the same thing for Julian. I'm already asking for a lot by moving in with him. His mom's a doctor, so I'm sure they help him with his bills, but that doesn't mean they're wealthy.

I'm not even sure if his parents have money. His mom may be a doctor and his dad is a deputy sheriff, but they both work in a small town. It's great and honorable work, but I'm guessing the pay isn't great.

All that Julian has to offer me is himself, and that's all I want. Still, I have even less to offer him. I'm an unemployed young girl who reads kinky romance books and who is aiming for a cosmetology degree and pining away for a man too old for me.

A soft knock disturbs my rapidly unfocused thoughts. "Come in."

"So, are we going to talk about how you got what you wanted?" my mother asks, smiling at me. I just rushed past her after Julian walked out. My excitement was a little too much to control.

I grin back, turning myself around and plopping down on my bed. "I suppose I did."

"Don't sound modest, now."

I bounce on my bed, thrilled to the gills about a chance to live with Julian. "Fine, you have me there. I want it more than anything, but it's only the beginning, and you know it. He has to want me, too."

"You know he does."

"You think so, but it's been several years, and he has done everything he can to avoid seeing me—and when he does, he's a total big brother, a big jerk."

My mother rolls her eyes and shakes her head as she walks over to me, gently taking my hands in hers. "Sweetie, we've been through this. The man is obsessed with you and is only holding back because you're Drake's little sister and you were underage."

"Yes, and now that I'm an adult, he hasn't even bothered to make a move."

"You're still Drake's little sister. Convince him that he's better off crossing that line than not. If he's not willing to choose you over your brother, then maybe he isn't the guy for you," my mom adds. That's the part I've considered all this time. Yes, he might find me attractive, but if it's just looks, then he may not be willing to ruin his friendship for a fling.

"Thanks, Mom. I don't want to force him to want me, but I can't miss this opportunity. Are you sure you're making the right decision with Harold?" I take her hands in mine, giving them a squeeze.

She looks me deep in the eyes. "Yes. He's a good guy. He's not like the other ones. Sometimes you have to kiss a lot of frogs. And if your father was still alive, there wouldn't be any other frogs for me."

"I'm sorry, Mom." We hug, and when I pull away, I try to lighten the mood. "Oh, Mom, I wanted to ask about my bed. Will I be taking it?"

"I don't see why not. We'll get you a moving truck and maybe con your new roommate to help, along with his brothers."

"I think that's asking way too much."

"If not, we'll get movers. It's not a lot of stuff, but I already have movers coming for the rest of the house, so they'll be busy packing everything up."

"Okay."

"Get some rest." I nod, and she gives me a great big squeeze before getting up and leaving my room.

"I CAN'T THANK YOU ENOUGH FOR DOING THIS AGAIN," Drake says on the phone as Julian drives me to his apartment. Well, now "our" apartment.

"Yeah, no problem," he grunts a perfunctory reply.

"Look, I've got to go. Everly, don't give him trouble, and Julian, make sure you keep every dick away from her."

28

"No problem," he growls before ending the call.

"You know, neither of you own my body. I'm twenty, not a minor. If I want to have sex, I can."

"You can't be fucking in my damn home, and I'm going to explain something to you. If a man really wants you, he's not going to take you in the back seat of a vehicle, so don't go buying that bullshit, Everly."

"Holy shit, you know my name," I say, surprised. I think that's the first time I've heard it.

"Must you be a pain in my ass already? If you keep it up, I can find a place for you somewhere else."

I freeze, feeling my heart crack. The thought of him tossing me out so effortlessly hurt. "I'm sorry," I mutter, looking out the window so he can't see the way my eyes fight the tears in them.

He huffs. "Everly." I expect him to say something, but then his phone rings. I see the caller ID on the dashboard display. It's Dallas General.

"This is Dr. Martinez."

"We're sorry, Dr. Martinez, but we need you to come in."

"Yes, I'll be in shortly. Give me an hour and a half."

"Thank you, sir." He ends the call and then he takes my hand, giving it a gentle squeeze.

"Don't worry. My brother Rick and my cousins will be around to help you move in." He quickly releases it as I nod. We pull up to a small apartment building, and he backs into a parking space. As we exit the vehicle his brother walks up to us. "Hey," he says, greeting me with a chin nod.

"Are we ready to unload?" Julian asks Rick.

"We already started, bro."

"Really?" I look in the truck, and I don't see my bed. If it was the last thing they loaded, then it should be the first thing to come out.

"Come on—I'll show you the place, although I'm sure you've already seen it before."

"No, I haven't." He snaps his head back. "Drake never let me come here before."

"Really?"

"I guess he had his reasons. Like I said, he doesn't want me to cramp his style with the chicks. I should have brought a bunch of disinfectant." I scrunch up my face at the thought of all the gross bodily fluids left in the room. Maybe this is a bad idea.

"That could be the reason. Don't worry. The room has been cleaned and disinfected." Julian pulls a smile out on one side of his lips. I didn't think it was possible around me. Maybe this won't be completely horrible. Then again, that little bitty twist of his lips adds to his beauty.

"Thank you."

"No problem. He's my best friend, but his habits were a bit much."

"Yes, they were." I choke out a laugh. "That's an understatement." Julian smirks as he grabs a big box like it weighs absolutely nothing and carries it into the apartment. We walk in, and I'm surprised that despite the men moving in and out, the place is immaculate and huge.

"There's a lot of space for you to study. You can use that desk over there. I have a private office in another room. Your brother used that one there." He nods toward a medium wooden desk in the corner of the room.

I'm not sure I'll need it, but I thank him for being so kind. "Oh, thank you."

"Now, this way to your bedroom." He takes the lead, and it gives me a moment to observe his handsome figure from behind. Goodness, what the hell does he do when he's not busting his tail at the hospital because the man is muscular. From head to toe, it's visible even through his clothes. His black tee fits like a second skin, perfectly formed to his frame, making my mouth water.

"This one is mine. We have separate bathrooms, thank goodness." His tone and snark instantly offend me and even hurt my feelings, if I'm being honest with myself.

"Damn, I'm not a messy girl," I hiss, crossing my arms.

"I was talking about your brother, but I have four siblings. It can be crowded. I believe a house should have as many bathrooms as bedrooms."

"Are you serious?"

"Yes. You've never seen a house where everyone has to be somewhere at the same time. Pure chaos."

"How many girls?"

"Luckily, just my mom and my sister, but don't underestimate us men. We can take up the bathroom for a long time."

"Gross. Jerking off too much can make you go blind."

"I have perfect vision, brat."

"Yeah, and he sure as hell beat that thing like it owed him money," Rick said, walking past us.

"Fuck off."

"You're the champ. Hey, princess, where do you want all these boxes?"

"I have no idea."

"Come look at your room, and then you can unpack. I have to leave in ten minutes," Julian says.

I step inside the room that once belonged to Drake, and I'm floored. It's not what I expected. The walls are pale pink, and the dressers are white. What's most shocking is the bed in the corner of the massive room isn't mine. "Oh, no. You didn't leave my brother's bed, did you?"

"No, my mother picked it out. She thought you could use a new one."

"I can't afford it."

"Call it a housewarming present."

"I can't believe it." I look at the headboard, and it's a beautiful white padded board with a quilted pattern.

"Our mom loves doing things like this," Rick says.

A growl comes from Julian. "Can I have a word with you?" He stares at his brother.

"Sure." They step out of the room and walk down the hall while I take in the room. It's gorgeous. It's pretty much a blank canvas for me to decorate. I can't believe they painted the walls of the apartment.

I shoot my mom a message telling her that I'm here and that I'm unpacking.

"Hey—Julian had to leave and we'll be getting out of here shortly, but if you need anything before we go, just let us know. Also, there is some food in the fridge. My mom dropped off a lasagna for Julian."

"Thank you." I'm sad that Julian didn't bother to say goodbye, but I know he has to work. About fifteen minutes later, Rick and the other guys leave the apartment, handing me the keys and telling me that Julian left the passcode on the fridge.

I walk into the kitchen and take a look around. Seriously, this looks like a well-established doctor's pad, not a resident's place. I love it, but damn, how can they afford it? I'm going to have to get a job and chip in. My brother must have given Julian a pretty penny for this place. I can't let him continue to foot the bill.

I run my hand over the pristine counter and sigh. "What am I going to do?" I mutter. Suddenly, I feel completely out of my realm. I have class tomorrow, so I wonder if I'll see Julian. This is going to be interesting.

My brother said their paths crossed more at the hospital than they did at the apartment so I'll be happy to have privacy, but he also said that I should heed Julian's warning about the boys or I'll find myself homeless. I don't doubt it because I'm already annoying him.

I hate lasagna, so I don't touch it. There's something about thick noodles that makes my stomach turn. Still, beggars can't be choosers. I need a job to feed myself. The fridge is damn near empty, so I need to find something or I'll be hard swallowing a plate of pasta. Digging into the cabinets, I pull out a box of granola bars and snag one before heading to the bedroom and working on my many, many boxes.

I don't know when I passed out, but I wake up in the middle of my bed with half of the boxes opened and put away. It was well after midnight when I last looked at my phone, but Julian hasn't come home. It's already ten in the morning, and I need to head to class.

Thankfully, my mom and brother hooked me up with a bus card. I step outside the house with my card in hand and my book bag on when Julian pulls up. "Hey, where are you going?"

"To school," I say. "Are you just getting back from work?"

"Yes. Get in, and I'll give you a ride."

"Aren't you tired?"

"Yes, so get in so I can come back and get some sleep." I don't want to argue with him because frankly, I miss him. When I open the truck door, I smell nothing but Julian and the fresh car scent. I breathe it in and sigh.

"Thanks. I wasn't looking forward to the new route to school."

"No problem. I have another car for you to use for school."

"Thanks, but I'm good. I have a bus card."

"What did I say?"

"Look, I don't have a job yet, which means gas money isn't just flowing out of my pockets. My mom only gave me so much." When I was living at home, she didn't want me to work because she wanted me to focus on school, and since my tuition was paid off by a scholarship, I didn't have to work. Now, it's a must.

I remember the restaurant job. Ugh. I hated that place. The boss was so handsy that my bestie and I made up an excuse for me to call off, but then my mom came to me and said my boss fired me for not coming in. I promised to find another job, but she just wanted me to focus on school.

"Don't worry about it. I'll fill it up. It's safer for you, and I want to keep my promise to Drake." Despite being a douche, my brother has always been protective of me. I later found out that Drake had gone down to the restaurant and punched that guy in the face for touching me. I don't know how they found out, but he took care of it.

"You don't have to take it that seriously. The apartment was more than enough."

"No, it isn't. Look, Everly, I'm tired, and today was a rough one. Can you not argue with me about this?"

"Of course." I press my hand to his and say, "I'm sorry. I don't mean to be ungrateful. You have been nothing but generous to me."

"You're not, but I expect you to do what I say the first time."

"Yes, Daddy," I mutter under my breath.

"Would you care to repeat that?" His voice grows stern, and my panties are soaked.

"Nope."

"That's what I thought." He pulls the car over, and that's when he adds, "We're here."

"Wow, that was fast." How did he know where my school was? Did Drake tell him? Probably gave him all my damn information. My brother said that Julian was a straight arrow and completely by the book, so he studied everything. He probably has my social security too.

"Thank you," I say.

"I work again in eight hours. What time do you get out?"

"I don't get out until four."

"Oh, well, someone will be here to pick you up."

"Are you serious?"

"Of course I am. Have a good day in class." I get out and go to class, hoping that he doesn't have someone else go out of their way.

CHAPTER THREE

JULIAN

IT'S BEEN A WEEK. ONE WEEK, AND I'VE ONLY SEEN HER THREE times. Each time has been a blessing and pure torture as well. She looks perfect in my place, but she'd look better in my bed with my last name as hers.

My phone rings as I pull into my parking space at the apartment. "Hello," I answer.

"Hey, brother," Drake says.

"How's it going in Seattle?" I ask since I haven't heard from him since he left.

"It's fucking fabulous. I'd tell you to come up here for all the women, but that's pointless because you didn't take advantage of the ones you had there." God, is he watching me? Does he know how bad I want to take advantage of his little sister?

"Always about women," I sigh.

"Are you gay? You can tell me. I'm your friend, and I'm in the most liberal city around. Trust me —there's nothing wrong with it. It can be pretty nice to have a guy go…"

"Hey, hey. No, I'm not gay, and I don't want to hear about your sexual escapades. I'm just waiting for the right woman and the right time."

"Wow, okay. So anyway, how is my sister doing? Driving you insane yet?"

"Not too much, but then again, like I told you before, I don't see her that often. I'm working all hours, and she's doing her school thing."

"Plus, she's got a job now too. I've sent her some money because she didn't have any food."

"No food? Son of a bitch. I hadn't thought about any of that. She got a job?"

"Yeah, she got one two days ago. She needed money to survive now, unlike before when my mom was buying groceries and stuff, but it's not like it's your responsibility to feed her. I asked you to give her a place to stay." What the fuck? I had no damn idea.

"Still, I would have made sure she was fed or at least gotten groceries in the house. Yeah, I guess I hadn't talked to her. I'm glad I lent her my other car, then."

"Thanks for that, by the way. I hate the idea of her taking

the bus around Dallas in the middle of the night." She's not going to be doing that at all.

"Where is she working?" I ask.

"At the mall food court."

"Well, it looks like she's not home right now, but I'm about to go inside and eat before going to sleep. I'll talk to you later."

"Get some sleep, and thanks again for looking out for Everly. She's everything to us."

"No problem." I end the call and exit my truck, feeling like an asshole because I want nothing more than to sink my teeth into Everly and bury my cock deep inside her. Drake wouldn't understand what his sister does to me. I'm twisted in my desire for her. It's fucking great that I'm constantly busy and don't have time to dwell on the urge to fuck her tight little hole.

When I enter the apartment, it smells good. I walk over to the kitchen and see a note on the counter. *I went to the store. I needed some ingredients for dinner.*

Just as I set the note down, the door unlocks. My head turns, and in walks Everly, looking beautiful with too many damn bags in her hands. "Everly, what are you doing carrying all that?"

"No second trips," she says, giving me a wink and a grunt. I rush over and snag them all from her. Some of them are too damn heavy.

"Next time we'll go to the store together, or I can do it. That shit is too heavy for you to be carrying."

"I'm not a weakling, Dr. Martinez."

"I know, but I'm supposed to be taking care of you, and I apparently haven't been doing a very good job." I cup her chin. "How long have you been going around without eating?"

"Who told you that?"

"Drake just called me."

"It hasn't been that bad. Honestly, I snagged some granola bars you had in the cabinet, a bit of the meals your mom left, except the lasagna—not a fan of pasta. Besides, my new job gives me one free sandwich at the end of my shift. So, I have had one meal twice this week for free." She winks.

"No more with the starving bullshit. If you're fucking hungry, you tell me, okay?"

"Um…"

"Don't dare try to argue with me, little girl. Just do me a favor and say, 'yes.'"

"Yes, Daddy."

"God, you're a brat."

She bounces on her toes with a smile. "True, but I have to cook so we don't starve and so you can get some sleep."

"Do you need some help?"

"No."

"Okay. Well, I'm going to hop into the shower."

"It should be done in about half an hour." I nod and walk away, avoiding the desire to taste her lips. My body aches to pull her into my arms. Still, I resist and head into my bedroom for a hot shower. I need to wash off the gross day and the lingering filthy thoughts I have of Everly, although I'm not sure how much good that will do since we actually have time to spend together.

I undress and toss my clothes in the hamper, which is full, reminding me that I need to do laundry tomorrow since it's my day off. When I step inside, the hot water feels good against my skin, and I let out a deep groan. After squeezing the last of the soap onto my washcloth, I realize I'm going to need to run to the store. Perhaps Everly needs some items as well.

My hand lingers over my length that stiffens as Everly's name comes to mind. I tell myself to get control and stop, but knowing that she's in the kitchen, making me dinner, only arouses me more. I drop the cloth and wrap my fist around my thick cock, giving it a squeeze before stroking it from base to tip. A groan falls from my lips as I close my eyes.

"Everly," I grunt, stroking myself up and down.

"Fuck. That's right—open that smart mouth of yours." She does, giving me her doe eyes full of mischief as she parts her lips. I slip my fat head between them and groan as she sucks in the tip. "Good girl. Suck my cock like you have been begging for." She continues, choking on it and then pulling off.

"So big, Daddy."

"Give Daddy what he wants," I growl, stuffing it back in her mouth, fucking her pretty throat. I fist her hair and say, "I'm about to come, and you're going to swallow." She moans around my girth with a smile around her eyes. I pump my hand faster and groan her name as I come, shooting it all over the shower floor and wall.

I quickly wash up and rinse off, remembering that she's in the kitchen. I get dressed in some joggers and a tee shirt, sliding it over my head and down my chest as I enter the kitchen.

"Damn, it smells good in here."

"Thank you," she says, staring at my body. Fuck, my dick jerks right back to life, so I hurriedly take a seat on one of the stools at the kitchen island. "Hopefully you enjoy it." She plates the dish, and my mouth is watering as she bends forward, her tits practically on display.

"I'm sure I will. Your brother said you were a great cook." I take a bite of the food, and it's incredible. A moan escapes my throat, and I look up from my plate to see her pretty, light brown eyes on me. "Your brother was right. You are fantastic. This is a wonderful braised beef and veggies dish."

"Thank you." Her cheeks turn a rosy pink as her fork stalls mid scoop.

"Go on and eat. I'd hate for it to go cold." We eat in companionable silence, and I ache for her even more. This is what I want with her. The way I can look across the table and see her enjoying her meal, stealing glances every so often.

"So, how is this job that you forgot to mention?"

"To be fair, it's not like I see you around often enough."

"It is fair. So, how is it?"

"What can I say? It's a job…at the mall…working in the food court. There's nothing special about it in the least, but hey, I can't complain because I need the money."

"You don't need the money."

"The heck I don't. No offense, but I already don't pay any bills, and I can't have my brother send money to me when he's not making bank yet. I'm no mooch."

"I get it, little girl. Don't get heated. What I'm saying is that you can just earn your keep here." Her brows kick up with a twist of her lips. I wonder if she's thinking something filthy, but as much as I'd love to have her in my bed, I'd never demean her like that.

"Come on. You just proved to me that you can cook. I can see that you keep the house clean, and frankly, I'm extremely busy. So, I can pay you to keep the house clean, including my room and the laundry. Also make sure I have my meals prepared for work."

"What type of meals are you talking about?"

"Don't freak out. I'm not a full-dinner-every-day kind of guy. I love a good sandwich and chips for work." She twists her lips as she contemplates my offer. I think it's a fair one.

"I don't think it's right taking your money since I live here for free already."

I try to think of a way to put it. As my wife, she'll get my money and do those things anyway. At least until she has her certification and gets the position she wants, and then we'll share the tasks. "Well, just think of it as a live-in housekeeper," I suggest.

I watch the wheels turn in her head. "When you put it that way…I suppose it makes sense."

"So how does that sound?" I'm hoping that she says yes because it's a lot easier to keep an eye on her if she's in the house. The cameras are all around the house and on the exterior. The ones in the car are good too. I've already asked my brothers to do me a favor and try to keep an eye on her while she's coming and going from class, but they didn't have any idea that she had a damn job. Now, I'm going to have to find someone else to keep tabs on her if that's the case. She has no notion about how serious I am about her safety. Until she moves to Steeleville, I'm taking her safety to the next level.

"I'm on a trial basis at the food court anyway, so I guess this would be better," Everly says.

"Good. Your brother will be happy about it." We finish

dinner, and then I help her with the dishes. As she scrubs, I toss dishes in the dishwasher.

"Thank you for dinner again." I lean in and give her a gentle peck on the cheek. It's a dumb move and I regret it immediately, so I excuse myself and say, "Goodnight. I'm exhausted."

"Goodnight, Jules." She dries her hands and then turns off the light.

It's the next morning when I'm doing my laundry that I find her clothes in the dryer. "Fuck," I groan. My dick throbs in my sweats as I pull her panties out of the pile and bring them to my nose. They're freshly laundered, but I don't care because they're hers. Does that make me twisted? Maybe. Do I fucking care? No. "Hey, I thought I was supposed to be taking care of that?"

My back straightens, and I drop them back into the pile. "Well, I figured you'd quit your job first before you jump on all the tasks. Besides, I have a lot of clothes to handle."

"Of course." She steps beside me and then grabs the basket, pulling her clothes out of the dryer. "How often do you do your clothes?"

"I have one day off a week, so I try to get it done within two weeks. Usually both my hampers in my bathroom and bedroom are overflowing by then."

"Okay. Well, I'll check the hamper twice a week. How is that?"

"Sounds great," I say, feeling like a damn slob. "I have to go to the store in a bit. Is there anything else we need?"

"I'm not sure, exactly, because it will depend on what you want to eat."

"Well, how about we get this started and then go together?"

"I think that's a good idea."

Twenty minutes later we're dressed and ready to go. She hops in my truck, and the damn air is sucked out of the vehicle. Maybe we should have taken the sedan, which has just a little more breathing room. Damn it, the lack of space feels so confined.

"So how is school?" I ask, trying to distract myself.

"It's great. I'm killing it, as you can see." She palms the bottom of her hair, and it bounces like a spring. I love the color and the way the light shines off it. Damn, could she be any more perfect? This wasn't meant to be a bonding moment, but I can't help myself.

"So, are you on call today, or is it your actual day off?"

"It's my day off," I say, turning my head to peek at her.

"That sucks," she mutters.

"Why?"

"Because you're going to the store instead of just relaxing." Spending time with her is still better than anything else. I should be keeping my distance, but I can't help myself. All I know is that being around Everly is addictive.

"I know. That's why I'm hoping that you can start making it a little easier. It's crazy how much the little mundane tasks become time wasters."

"Right? The little things take too much time. You need more days off. Will you get more soon?"

"Next year when I finish my residency, I'll be moving to Steeleville and working at the Medical Center there."

"Until then, you work in Dallas?"

"Yes, and I'll have to find a place in Steeleville. It's not like it's a huge town. There are apartment buildings that are already rented, and I'm waiting to buy a house. The drive there is only forty-five minutes." She doesn't realize that I'm staying here for her. I actually can stay with my parents until I have a house that I want.

"Oh, well. I hope that's not for at least four months."

"I have ten more months on this lease."

"Well, that's good for me." It's a little white lie, but I don't want her to feel like a burden.

"Come on. We're here." It takes us about two hours to shop and get back to the house.

My phone rings, so I excuse myself to speak with my father while she makes lunch.

CHAPTER FOUR

EVERLY

IT'S BEEN A FULL MONTH, AND THINGS HAVE MOVED smoothly between us. When it comes to being roommates, we glide like butter—perfectly smooth. There isn't any friction to be had, and maybe that's because I haven't crossed the line after quitting my cashier gig.

My job didn't even care that I left because there was another person looking for a job that same day. They never take the sign down because young kids have a hard time juggling school and work. I thanked them for the opportunity and collected my check. Julian even waited for me in the mall parking lot to ensure I wasn't upset after I told the manager. He wanted to go in with me, but I told him no. "Look, I'm a big girl and I can handle myself."

"Yeah, and what if he shouts at you? What are you going to do?"

"What are you going to do?" I challenged Julian.

"Give him a reason to visit me at the hospital," he answered. Damn, why is that so sexy? He's just acting like my big brother demanded. Still, I loved seeing the way his eyes darkened when he promised to slay my dragons.

"Yeah, don't break your oath over nothing, Doctor. I'm going to be all right." I gave him a wink and handled the matter quickly and with little to no trouble.

In the days afterward, Julian and I go back to our usual routine of seeing each other in passing and then the occasional lunch and our weekly grocery run followed by a call to my brother where I try to send my brother the money, but he tells me to just save it.

The money in my bank account has been steadily growing as it is. I hardly use it for groceries because Julian takes me grocery shopping on his days off and pays for them. Most of my money goes to gas for the car and the occasional odds and ends.

Guilt fills me because it feels like I'm using Julian for his money. It's the most I've had in my account in a long time for no reason. Julian isn't around making a big mess, so I'm pretty much cleaning up after myself, which I need to get started on.

Today is another day of cleaning and cooking before my afternoon class. It starts at two, so I have plenty of time. I think about my schedule and look at my calendar. Julian isn't supposed to be here until four today, so I have time to get some chores done without getting in his way and I can make his lunch for tomorrow.

Sliding on my headphones, I get to work on the laundry, starting with his first. I enter his bedroom to grab his hamper and take it to the laundry room, and then I come back to the bathroom to grab the second hamper. When I open the door, I let out a gasp that I catch with my hand to my mouth. Julian is home, and he's hung like a damn horse.

I swiftly and gently close the door, hoping I didn't get spotted. I'd die of mortification if Julian saw me gawking at his beautifully sculpted body with his huge cock that he had firmly in his hand. Without paying attention to where I'm going, I continue to back up, and I fall onto his bed. "Shit." I bounce off like it's a spring and dash out the door, closing it with a little less finesse than I should have.

Darting to the laundry room, I catch my breath while leaning against the washer. My heart drums against my ribcage, beating wildly. Even as I ran out, I wanted to run right back in and get another peek at that handsome specimen. Damn, Julian is gorgeous.

The song in my headphones switches, startling me, and I nearly fall sideways. Straightening up, I start the laundry and dump the load in the washer after checking all the pockets.

Once everything is sorted and the machine is running, I walk into the kitchen to begin lunch. As I work on the meal, my mind goes straight to the explicit sight I encountered.

Julian's gorgeous figure was draped in sheets of water as he took his length in hand, eyes closed, groaning. Soap lathered his skin, acting as lube for his hand as he worked it up and down the shaft. My thighs slam together, pussy throbbing hard as the image plays in my head. It was a fast glimpse, but I swear the memory is branded on my mind.

I can't shake it, but I have to cook and pretend everything is normal. I take out the mushrooms, tomatoes, and zucchini from the fridge and rinse them before setting them on the counter to be chopped. The door to the bedroom opens and I drop the containers, scattering the vegetables all over the kitchen floor.

"Shit."

"Whoa," Julian says, catching a rolling zucchini. My eyes land on his large hand wrapped around the zucchini, and a wave of heat floods my face.

"Um...sorry," I stammer, looking up from the floor to meet his gaze.

"It's okay," he says, smirking. "A little dirt never hurts." He stands, and then I get a full view of him in a pair of dark jeans and his bare chest. Goodness, looking that good should be a damn crime. He puts the vegetables back in the colander to be washed again.

I start cutting the vegetables and then he says, "I set the

hamper in the laundry room." The knife slips in my hand, and I cut my finger.

"Ah," I scream. "Fuck," I mutter, dropping the knife onto the counter. I'm off to the sink to rinse my finger, and Julian is right behind me. I feel his body brush up against my back.

"Damn it, baby. What did you do? Let me see it." I fight the stinging tears in my eyes. Did he just call me baby? I turn slightly to give him room to view my wound. It's bleeding as Julian pulls it away from the water, but it's not too terrible. When he takes my hand, suddenly the pain dwindles and my heart races. "You're not going to need stitches, but I need to get my kit. Give me a minute." He opens a kitchen drawer and pulls out the bandages. My body tingles, and my pulse picks up as he works on me. Being around Julian has that effect.

"It feels better already," I say, peeking through my lashes.

"That's good. You have to be careful, sweetheart. As much as I like my meat bloody, I can skip the blood in my vegetables."

"Ha, ha," I snark, sneering at him briefly before hissing as he wraps my finger.

"Sorry. It's all better now. I'll finish this, and you take a seat." He points to the uncut veggies.

"It's my job," I remind him.

He glares at me, but that look doesn't have the effect he thinks it does. My entire being wants to jump into his arms. "Just sit your little bratty ass down and relax. I can cook, okay?"

"Are you sure? Your mom brings all your meals, or I've made them," I remind him.

"Well, I can at least chop," he confesses with chagrin. He tosses the ruined vegetables and cleans all the utensils and the cutting board. "At least I'm good at cutting others and not myself, little brat," he mocks, sticking his tongue out at me.

Damn, he looks great in the kitchen, but I can't let him do all the work, so I bargain with him. "Okay. How about you chop, and I handle the cooking part?"

"I'll agree to that." I hop off the stool and move to the stove. He smiles and tosses me a wink, which damn near makes my knees buckle. I take a pan from the cabinet and prepare it with olive oil while he gets the remaining vegetables together.

"Good, because haven't you heard you shouldn't cook without a shirt on? As a doctor, you should know better." I wag my bandaged finger in his handsome face. "You also forgot the magic treatment too." He leans in and kisses my finger.

"Is it all better?" Our bodies are a little too close, breathing growing heavy.

"It's a start," I whisper, my lips parting as I ache to taste his hardened, stubbled jaw that is just inches from me.

The pan behind me starts to sizzle. "You should get that."

"Yeah." I turn around and turn it down, beginning to make the dish. I refuse to look at him again while I'm cooking so he can't see how flushed my face is.

CHAPTER FIVE

JULIAN

I'M SO GRATEFUL THAT LUNCH IS OVER. I SET THE DISHES IN the dishwasher, thanking Everly before excusing myself because my phone begins to ring. "Hello, Mom."

"Hey, sweetheart. What time are you coming over?"

"I'll be there in about an hour. I was getting ready." I give Everly a sheepish smile, feeling like I'm abandoning her even though I don't owe her an explanation for where I'm going or who I'm going with. It's been a while since I visited with my family, and I promised that I'd come over. There is a big gathering at the clubhouse today, and with the weather playing nicely, we should have a good turnout of Steele Riders and their kin.

Besides, I have to get away from Everly before I do something stupid. Hell, I already did something stupid; kissing her finger was reckless.

Every bit of the meal was like a ticking time bomb. Most of it we sat in silence, each of us aware of the growing tension, the heat hotter than the summer sun, and when she lifted the damn fork to her lips, I wanted to toss it on the floor and take her on the table. Everything I do has been crazily pushing boundaries beyond necessary. She is driving me wild.

I'd been in the shower and stroking my cock, knowing damn well she was down the hall. Hell, I put the laundry basket in the room because I saw she took the hamper away. She must have realized I was in the shower, which means she could have heard me saying her name over and over again as I came. Is that why she cut herself?

"Hey, Drake. Yeah, Julian's right here, but he's about to leave." I slam my eyes shut as I tuck my wallet in my pocket.

"He's always on the run," she continues with a giggle. "Okay, I'll tell him." She ends her call and approaches me.

"What's up with Drake?" I grunt.

"He's good, but he said he called you over the past couple of days and you haven't called him back."

"Shit. Yeah. So why did the asshole hang up? When I'm busy, I get distracted, and he knows that."

I shake my head and pull out my cell phone to call my best friend back so he can stop being a whiny little bitch and I can stop feeling guilty about avoiding him because I want to smash his little sister. "Hey, Drake. How's it going?"

"It's great. I'm loving this place, and I'm trying to convince your ass to come and join me."

"Not going to happen. You know I love it here and wouldn't leave no matter what."

"Fine. Well, that's not the only reason I'm calling. Are you standing close to Everly?" he asks in a conspiratorial whisper.

"Yeah, why?" I answer, taking a peek in her direction before moving my gaze toward the window.

"Well, I wanted to talk to you about her."

"Okay, give me a minute." I walk off to my bedroom and close the door. "What's up?"

"Nothing too bad, but I'm not liking the friends she has. They're trying to get her in trouble, and my mom told me she's into some guy so bad that she'll end up knocked up soon. She didn't say who, only that she's crushing hard."

"I haven't seen her with anyone," I growl.

"That's good, but then again, you have rules so if she's seeing someone, it's when they're not at your place." Fuck, he had a point. Is my brother not doing his damn job? I know he's only following her to and from school, but there are moments when she's out with friends. I need someone to keep tabs on her then. Employing some of the prospects for that job is a must.

"You don't know who this asshole is?" I ask. There's a severe pain in my chest at the notion that she's seeing some guy. She deserves someone special, and the fact that no one is good enough for her doesn't help. Frankly, I'm the only one for her.

"No, but it's probably someone she's seeing from school. I'm just worried about her getting knocked up. She's old enough to date, even if I don't like it."

"You've changed your mind quickly about her dating."

"Well, she's twenty, Julian. I just don't like the idea of bastards acting like me or her acting like my mom and falling head over heels for fucking dumb punks who aren't worth her time or who end up getting her pregnant. What happens if she doesn't finish her certification first or doesn't get a decent gig? My mom fell into that trap and struggled. I don't want to see Everly make the same mistake."

He has a point. She would struggle, but not if she were mine because not only would she finish, but I would help her any way I could. I have a trust fund that can cover our needs for the rest of our lives, not to mention my earnings as a doctor. I'm sure she'll earn a lot as a stylist. She's shown me her work, and it's good. I've even allowed her to give me a haircut. From now on, no one else will be allowed to cut my hair.

Besides, he has a lot of room to talk. He's out there banging anything that walks. He's lucky that he hasn't knocked anyone up. His residency is up, but he's got student loans and a long time before he's making a killing.

"I understand. What do you want me to do? I'm about to head out."

"See if you can find out who this fuck is." That is something I sure as hell will do for my own sake.

"I'll see, but you're probably closer to finding out."

"You're probably right," he chuckles. "Have a good one, and maybe I can get you to change your mind and choose a position up here. Although, I hope it's after my sister gets hired down there."

"Still not happening, but nice try."

"Fine. Take care, and try talking to her about being safe, at least. I'm not interested in having the safe-sex talk with her." I sure the fuck ain't interested in that talk. The only safe sex talk I'm having with her is to keep a motherfucker safe from me. They better keep their dicks far away from her before I kill them. The thought of any man sniffing around her sets my teeth on edge.

I'm the only bastard who can be sniffing around her.

I'm glad we didn't have that damn discussion before I left because I wouldn't have been able to leave before I found out who the asshole is who's caught her interest. Angry and full of jealousy, I ride my motorcycle fast, too fucking fast through traffic, and make it to Steeleville in short order.

She's young, and men would be stupid not to be hitting on her like crazy.

Everyone is there when I get to the clubhouse. They greet me, but they're looking around suspiciously. My father meets me with a strong, one-armed hug. "Hey, Pops. It's good to see you. How are you?"

"Hey, Mijo. It's good to see you. Still running from your wife?" he chuckles, looking around me to see if I'm hiding Everly.

"She's not my wife," I grumble.

"But you want her to be."

"Yes, but have you considered she doesn't? Fuck, I just found out that she's probably seeing someone. Since I don't let anyone in my home, when she's not around she could be out fucking around."

"Where did you get that crazy idea from?"

"I spoke to her brother today, who told me that her mother said she's into some guy."

"Maybe you two need to talk."

"That's not as easy as you think. She's living with me, and what if she's not interested and I make her feel uncomfortable?"

"She doesn't want you? Has she given you any indication of that?"

"She doesn't want any of my money or help. She calls me old, and tells me I'm her father or something."

"Maybe it's because you boss her around like she's a kid instead of a woman," my sister says.

"Or maybe...she wants a good spanking," my other sister says, walking away with a wink.

"As gross as that is coming from Isabella, your sister might be right," my father mutters.

"She totally is. The early gray is totally giving Daddy vibes, cuz. Girls love a hot older guy," Beast's daughter says.

"What did you say, Wife?" Will growls.

She presses her hand to his chest, soothing him. "It's true. You need to see social media. It's everywhere, but you're my everything."

"Not into dudes, but thanks, sweetheart."

"I'm not getting old," I growl.

"No, but you're a lot older than her," Will adds. I want to kick his ass, but as he's the head of the Riders, that isn't a smart move. Besides, it would be a hell of a fight.

"Thanks for the reminder of why I've been staying away as much as I can and taking on more shifts than I need." After I finish my residency, I can cut it down to three shifts a week, but I want to build up a wall before I smash Everly on every damn surface of the apartment.

Will claps my shoulder and chuckles. "If that was a good reason, most of us wouldn't exist."

"Fair point," I grumble. I need a beer, and as if reading me like a book, my father hands me a cold one. "Thanks."

"Trust me. We've all been down this road, and Will can tell you that patience can pay off. Just don't be dumb and blow it by letting anyone else get in the way."

"I need someone watching over her when I can't."

"Are you afraid there's another guy, or are you're worried about her safety?" Will asks.

"A bit of both," I confess.

"Don't worry, cuz. I've got you. I'll have two guys at your disposal. Just put in the call, and we'll have them watch over her when needed."

"It shouldn't be often. As far as I can tell, she doesn't leave the apartment much, but when she does, it's with her one friend."

"Got it. I can make it happen. We have several prospects with shit all to do at the moment and are looking for an assignment, so this is perfect." I shake his hand and then follow my father out, who wants me to shoot some pool.

It's well after midnight when I get home and all the lights are off, so I carefully creep into the apartment, hoping that I don't disturb her.

There's a note on the dry erase board, which we got because it was easier than a notepad.

Dinner is stored in the green container for lunch tomorrow.

I smile to myself and then leave my own note just so she knows I saw it.

Thank you, baby girl.

After taking a piss, I walk to bed and strip down to my boxer briefs. I pull out my computer and bring up the footage from today. My eyes linger on her in the kitchen.

Then I remember that she could have seen me in the shower. I play it back and realize that she had her headphones in and was out of my bedroom quickly, so she probably didn't hear anything.

That's fucking good. I didn't need to embarrass myself like that. If she knew how damn much I stroke my cock from just the way she twirls her hair or from the sight of her at the stove, she'd run out of this apartment and demand her brother pick her up after he beats my ass, or at least tries to.

I set my laptop down and go to sleep since I have to work in the morning, but I don't get an ounce of rest because Everly is on my mind. Lately, she's always in my head.

Before, I could easily block her and focus on the goals I have because I felt like she was unattainable, a silly fantasy, but my family got into my head and now it's gotten out of hand. I have to be careful or Everly will be tied to my bed getting stuffed with my big cock, begging to be free or screaming for more, depending on who in my family is correct—my sister, or my cousin.

After my visit to Steeleville last week, I want to test my family's theory but I don't get a chance. I have to work nonstop and on my one day off, she has a full day of classes. Today we're both off, so I have something in mind. Besides, today's a special day, so as Everly enters the kitchen, I ask, "How are you feeling?"

"I'm fine. Why? Do I look crappy or something?" She huffs, slapping her hands on her hips.

"I'm asking about your finger," I answer with a smirk.

"Oh," she giggles. She pauses and then raises her injured finger to show me the new bandage. "Yeah, it still stings a little bit, but it's okay. I changed the bandage again yesterday, and it's almost completely healed."

"That's good. I'm riding out to Steeleville today. Do you feel like going for a ride?"

"Sure." She runs to her room and comes out a few minutes later dressed in a tiny pair of shorts and a tank top.

"Little girl, that's not going to work."

"It's hot out, and we're going to Steeleville. What's the big deal? Am I going to embarrass you or something?" I close the distance so that we're nearly touching.

"We're jumping on my Harley, baby."

Her mouth drops open. "I've never been on a bike before."

"Now is the time to learn."

Her pulse rises as I pin her to the edge of the sofa. I'm not sure it's the idea of riding or my closeness that has her heart rate spiked, so I step back. "I think it's a little far to learn."

"Don't worry. I'm not going to drop you."

"What if I let go?"

"Well, that would be dumb as hell. How about I give you a ride around here and see how you feel?"

"Okay." She bites on her bottom lip. The more this drags on, the more I think twice about doing this; having her little hands wrapped around my waist seems like a very dumb idea. Still, it's a family get-together for my birthday, and it feels wrong not to have her there.

"So, come on, little brat. Let's go." I turn her around and tap her bottom to send her on her way. Fuck, that was dumb as hell, but it felt so damn good.

"Okay, okay. You just literally told me two seconds ago." Everly waves me off and runs back to her bedroom to change, hopefully into something a little more practical.

She hurries up and puts on a pair of jeans that hug every inch of her ass and thighs, making those hips look absolutely delicious. I want to hold on to them and ride the fuck out of her until she is screaming my name. And I know it's wrong. I'm just about to head out when my phone rings, and it's Doc calling me.

"What's up, Uncle?"

"We need you at the hospital."

"Yeah, I'm on my way now."

"Nah, it's a serious situation at Dallas General. A building went down, and we need your help."

"I'm coming."

I end the call and tuck my phone in my pocket.

"Is something wrong?" Everly's soft voice questions with a hint of disappointment.

I turn back to Everly and apologize. "I'm sorry; we're going to have to cancel this outing. It seems I need to go to the hospital. There's an emergency. Maybe we'll try riding that bike another day."

"It's okay. I wasn't really thrilled about riding, anyway." I can read from her expression that she's being honest. "I hope everyone is going to be okay. Please be safe, Jules."

"I will." I give her a nod and then I head out, knowing that it's for the best. I'm playing a dangerous game with her. The more I'm around her, the more I'm going to give in. I keep wanting something I can't have, and it's silly and naive. When I get to the hospital, I find out that there was a construction accident, leaving two dead and twenty injured.

One of the guys who died had been a friend of mine that I went to school with. He left behind a family, and my heart aches for them. It's a fucking shame how life works out like that.

"Dr. Martinez, you did a tremendous job today," Nurse Suarez says.

"Thank you, Ms. Suarez."

"Call me Linda. If you need anyone to talk to or anything, I'm here for you." She presses her long nails on my arm, giving it a squeeze. "Wow, do you work out?"

"Yes, and I have plenty of people to talk to. Have a good night." I walk away, feeling more than irritated by her touch. That woman has had her eyes on me for months as soon as she realized that I was graduating at the top of my class.

"Do you want me to have her written up?"

"No, Mom. I'm an adult, and I don't need you to fight my battles like I'm still a little boy."

"No, but I am a hospital administrator, and I don't have to tolerate that bullshit. As a mother, I want to break her fingers. As a boss, I can fire her ass."

"Thanks, but I can handle it."

"Please tell me you're not having a thing…"

"God, no. You know that Everly is my only…"

"Well, then, what are you waiting for? I want grandbabies already, and you have more than enough money for it. Soon she'll be done with her program, have a certification, and there's a spot for her at the salon. The two of you can make pretty little babies for your father and me to spoil."

I kiss her cheek and shake my head. "I'll see you later."

"Don't forget about the event."

"I won't." We have a charity gala for the hospital in Dallas and I'd love to bring Everly, but I can't because there will be too many questions—too many doctors who know Drake and can get word to him in a heartbeat.

When I finally get home, I want to see Everly, but it's late and all the lights are off but a small one in the kitchen. There's something on the island: a birthday card and small wrapped present with a baked cake with blue icing. *Happy Birthday, Daddy.*

I open the card and laugh.

To the best dad ever. Happy birthday. I hope you get everything you want. Love your annoying little girl, Everly.

"What I want is your pussy on my face," I groan.

I open the gift and find a keychain that says the world's best dad. I'm going to spank the fuck out of her.

CHAPTER SIX

EVERLY

THE SECOND MONTH GOES BY WAY TOO FAST. JULIAN AND I hardly had a moment to spend together, and he grew even more distant. I'm in heaven and hell at the same time. I make his meals, and he's gone without a word most days. Maybe he hates my birthday presents. I'd gone out and got them after he disappeared. I had tossed out the other card I'd gotten him, and the tie I bought him is still in my drawer in the box. I was pissed that he left me after he'd bossed me around for the hundredth time.

Today he has a special dinner event with other physicians, and he comes out of his room in a fancy tuxedo. Of course, I'm nothing but a housekeeper, so he wouldn't even consider taking me as his plus one. He probably has a hot date that he's going to pick up before arriving at the gala.

God, my stomach burns at the image of some beautiful, elegant woman on his arm while I'm in my tee and shorts, lounging about, depressed and longing for a man who sees me as the teenage sister of his best friend even though I'm a grown woman now.

My mouth gapes wide open at his presence, but I rapidly catch myself and slam it shut before I let him know how attractive he is. "Wow, holy cow. You look handsome."

"Thanks."

The words slip from my mouth before I can think about it. "Remember, keep it down when you bring her home." It screams of pure jealousy, and he catches it.

He shakes his head and then smirks with his eyes smiling. "I'm not bringing anyone home."

I roll my eyes. "Whatever."

He closes the distance between us, causing my pulse to double. "Little girl, I'm going to a fancy event, but there's no reason to get jealous."

"I'm not jealous. I'm just looking out for you," I lie, staring at his broad chest in his fitted jacket that doesn't hide an ounce of his muscular frame. You'd think he was a gym bro the way he's so cut.

"Yeah, right," he growls, brushing his knuckles down my arm. A trail of goosebumps is left in its wake. So, he's on to me. He knows that I have a crush on him, and he's teasing me. I can't freaking believe he's being so cruel. Well, two can play that game.

My mood shifts, and I want him to pay for being a jerk. I lift my gaze to meet his and puff my chest. "Maybe I am jealous," I confess, pausing, and then add, "I'm jealous that I can't bring a boy home, so maybe I don't want you bringing anyone home."

His teeth clench together, jaw taut with tension. "I suppose that's fair."

Can I make him snap? He wants to tease me, put me on edge, knowing I have a crush, confusing me while going out to get some action. "If I have to go out to get my pussy eaten, you can t—" He moves so damn fast I don't have a chance to step back.

Julian's hand is around my throat, and his mouth is against my ear. "You better not have anyone touching, eating, or fucking your pussy." The way he says pussy causes my slit to drip onto my panties.

"I'm not," I say, hating how aroused I am and that he doesn't have any interest in me.

"Good. You better not be a bad girl."

"Or what?"

He pauses, and I wonder what punishment he'll threaten me with. The idea only arouses me more. "Your brother will be on our case," he growls with his beautiful blue eyes peering into mine.

I'm wondering if he's really using my brother as a buffer. "Of course not. My brother would be mad at you for not taking care of me."

"And you know I always try to do my best to take care of you. You're lucky I have to go because you were about to be punished." He lets me go and then walks out the front door without a backward glance. Still, even with him gone, I can feel the tension in the air.

My heart aches, and so does my body because there's no way I'm not going to be touching myself tonight. God, why does he do this to me? There is no way we're ever going to be a couple. The man runs hot and cold. Is it because of my brother, or my age? He seems like he wants me, but then he finds an escape. Our relationship has only gotten more complicated. He deposits money in my bank account every week, and then I take care of his meals and clothes.

Speaking of laundry, it's time to do a load or two. I walk into his bedroom and snatch the hamper, which is only half full. The one in the bathroom has even less, so I scoop out the clothes and carry them to the laundry room, only to find a piece of paper with a phone number and a woman's name written on it. "Of course," I sigh. He's fucking gorgeous. It's not his handwriting, but he kept it, so I set it on his dresser.

This is why. I'm not the kind of girl he can just sleep with and kick out of his bed. The connection with my brother makes it a problem. I decide that I need to get out of the apartment.

I've been invited to parties and stuff. There's no reason to stay home if he's going to be out with women, having fun.

Sitting on the sofa, I shoot off a text to my friend.

ME

Where is the party at?

KATE

Girl, we are at Joey's house. Big party.
Come on down.

ME

On my way in twenty.

I jump up and head over to the bedroom to find something sexy to wear. There's no way I'm going dressed in what I'm wearing right now. I'm not ready to go in this outfit.

It takes me about fifteen minutes to come out in a pair of jeans and a black one-shoulder top that cuts at my midriff. My hair is still partially curled from yesterday, but I still give it a quick run through with the curling iron and swipe on some makeup before turning everything off and running out of the apartment.

To be nice, I send Julian a message and let him know I'll be out.

ME

Hey, going out with friends.

JULIAN

No.

ME

Not asking for permission.

JULIAN

> You're asking for something. Can't you just behave?

ME

> I'm allowed to have friends.

JULIAN

> Be careful.

ME

> Okay. Don't screw anyone.

JULIAN

> You either. Or I'll rip their balls off.

ME

> Yes, Daddy.

CONTACT CHANGED FROM "JULIAN" TO "DADDY"

> Good girl.

My panties are ruined, but it's too late to turn back and change them, so I head to the party and when I get there, it's insanely loud. The people are spilling out onto the lawn, and I immediately regret my decision to go. I am looking for my friend Kate, and she's getting wasted with her boyfriend, Joey.

"Hey, girl. There you are," she squeals, jumping out of his arms. "God, you look hot. There are so many guys here, but I'm surprised you made it here without your guard dog breathing down your neck."

"He's at a business dinner."

"Still, he's always got someone watching you." She looks around me to see if there's anyone tailing me.

"No, he doesn't. You're crazy." I shake my head.

"Girl, there's always someone watching you. Right, Joey?"

He nods, taking another drink from his plastic cup. "Yup. I hope they don't bust up the party," he grumbles.

"I don't think so, since they have no idea where I am."

"Besides, how could they follow me?" That makes no sense, and I'm betting it's because they're drunk.

Suddenly, I hear the sound of police sirens going off.

"Fucking hell. I knew it, Kate. I told you it was a bad idea to invite her. Her fucking guard dogs called the police."

I'm stressed out because I'm going to be in trouble, and now my friends are pissed at me. The cops raid the house and break up the party.

I march out toward my vehicle, and as I'm about to grab the handle, I'm stopped by a cop. "Miss, before you drive off, you need to be tested for alcohol consumption."

"I haven't had anything to drink. I just arrived right before you pulled up."

"Then you'll have no problem taking a test." I glare at the woman on duty. I know it's not her fault that I'm at a frat party where everyone is getting wasted or that it got busted. Hell, I don't see anyone even watching me, but my friends swear that Julian has eyes on me.

"Fine." I take their test and pass, blowing a perfect zero. "Told you. Can I go now?"

"Yes."

"I'll see you later." I wave at Kate who is standing with Joey before going back to the apartment.

When I get home, Julian is standing in the doorway with his tux on, but his tie is gone and his arms crossed, accentuating his large muscles. The scowl on his face couldn't be any more severe if he tried.

"What are you doing here? Shouldn't you be trying to fight off the rich women clawing at your sleeves?" I challenge, wanting to fight with him. If what Kate said was true, this bust of a night is his fault.

"Get in the damn apartment now," he snarls, teeth clenched.

"Excuse me?" My head tilts to the side, my temper elevated.

"You heard me."

"What did I do wrong?"

"I got a call from my cop friend, informing me that my vehicle was at an illegal house party with a bunch of underage kids. I'm a fucking doctor, Everly. You know the risks of drunk driving, damn it," he roars.

I'm in his face. I breathe on him. "Does it smell like I was drinking?"

"No." I had no intention of drinking, but it seems like everyone just expects the worst of me, including the man I want the most.

"Goodnight," he mutters.

"Goodnight. Here are your keys. From now on, I'll take the damn bus to school, Dr. Martinez." I walk past him into the house. He reaches out for me, but I storm away and into my room, closing the door before he can react. As I strip out of my clothes, I hear him sigh and then finally walk to his room and close the bedroom door. It strikes me that he's home for the night. He came home for me.

I switch into a pale pink silk pajama short set and then wash off the makeup. He's in the shower, which means he's not asleep yet and I can apologize for making him come home early. As I head into his bedroom, I remember he has a load of laundry that I need to put away. I take it inside and set the basket down.

The phone number that was on the dresser is balled up in the empty trash. I scoop it out. "Wow."

I sit on his bed with the paper in my hand and stare at it. Who the fuck still writes their phone number on paper? I suppose it's still a thing, but...I hate whoever she is.

"What the hell are you doing in here?" he growls. I gasp and stare at him in just a towel wrapped around his tapered waist. Water beads down his chest, muscles are everywhere, and I can't look away. He's a true work of art that should be immortalized on walls, but then that would mean I'd have to share him, and I can't do it.

"Um...I came in here to apologize for making you come..." Damn it. I slap my hand over my mouth, giving myself away.

"What?" His brows shoot up, and I could swear something else jumped up too.

"I mean...I'm sorry that...you're mad at me."

"Mad at you? You have no idea what I am right now. Mad is just one thing, little girl."

"I'm not a little girl, and I'm allowed to go out and have fun."

He rushes toward the bed, tension in his entire body. His hand goes to my hair, fisting it. "Did you go to meet a boy?"

"No. Of course not," I answer, my lips parted. His other hand wraps around my throat while his thumb rubs my jaw. The tender rub of his thumb is in complete contrast to the tight grip he has on my hair.

"Who is Linda?" I question, opening my free hand and showing him the balled-up paper.

After a glance at it, I see the disgust on his face. "A nurse. I thought that was in the trash where it belongs."

"I found it on the floor and thought it was there by mistake." It was a lie, but I had to know more about it. Call it childish, call it what you will, but my heart is too fragile where Julian is concerned.

"No. So now that you've apologized; it's time for you to get your naked ass off my bed." He releases me and takes the paper, tossing it in the trash before opening his bedroom door.

"I'm not naked, Jules." He crosses his arms, causing his muscles to flex as he shakes his head at me.

"No, but you might as well be." He licks his lips as he stares right at my tits that are pebbled under the pink camisole.

"I could be if you wanted," I offer, running my finger under the thin strap of my top, teasing him. I'd give him anything he wants, and I can see how much he wants it. Every part of his body is screaming that he aches to fuck me: the way his eyes trail down my body, the lingering gaze on my breasts, and the huge bat he has ready to push through his towel.

CHAPTER SEVEN

JULIAN

"Get out of this room before bad things happen to you, little girl," I warn her, but the words go unheeded. The little temptress licks her plump lips in defiance.

"Julian, there isn't anything little about me." She runs one of her hands over her ample chest that's covered with nothing more than a tiny silk camisole. Her nipples underneath are already hardened to peaks as they press against the soft fabric, trying to tempt me. Her other hand slides over her hips, cupping her round ass. Fuck, I have to bite down on my bottom lip.

"The size of your hole and your waist are, and I promise you if you want to keep them that way, now is the time to leave." The thought of stretching out her pussy and watching her belly swell stiffen up my cock to a new, painful ache.

"I don't believe you, Jules. You're all talk."

"I'm a grown-ass man, Everly. You've just turned twenty." My heart races as I fight the inner battle to pin her to the bed and fuck her until neither of us can move or I let her escape.

She licks her finger and says, "Well, you're right, I'm legal, so I guess I'll just accept that date tonight. Don't wait up for me, Daddy." She moves to slide off the bed, and that's it. Battle over. She will never let another man come near her again.

"Daddy?" I play the word in my head because she's called me that so many times and I let it go before. Every time it gets harder and harder to ignore, and I don't know how I feel about that. It's bad enough that I'm already ten years older than her, but I'm not sure I need to be reminded of it. Fuck, since she moved in, I swear my new gray streaks have widened.

She nods. "Yeah, you're always telling me what to do. You won't let me have boys over, and you take care of almost all of my needs." She runs her hand over her pussy, and that's the last fucking straw.

"You shouldn't be here, and you should have quit your shit, but no. You didn't learn, little girl. Now it's too damn late. You've got me where you want me. You've broken me down until my leash has snapped and I'm free. I don't give a shit if your brother walked right in here. You messed up, little Eve." Everly is driving me insane.

"You want a lesson in what it's like to fuck with a grown man? This is what you get when you push too damn hard." I tug my towel free, letting the fucker fall to the floor, letting her see my nine-inch cock, semi-hard, filling back up after I just stroked myself raw to thoughts of just this. Now, I'm going to make it come to life.

Her mouth falls open, like she never imagined I'd make this move, but I'm not playing with her bratty ass anymore. No. Weeks of teasing me have come to an end. She isn't leaving this room without being stuffed with my cum.

"Get off my bed and get on your knees. I want you to suck my cock, little brat. I want to see those pouty lips that teased me with that lollipop this morning wrapped around me, sucking every drop of cum out of my dick." She hesitates. I haven't forgotten the way she slipped it passed her lips, slowly pulling it in and out so lazily while her tongue scored the underside.

"Julian," she gasps, sounding nervous and anxious as well. All of a sudden she's lost the bravado, but I'm done with the games. All thoughts are on fulfilling what we both need.

"Come on, now. Don't be shy after you damn near broke down my door to get a peek at me stroking my cock. Get over here and take care of what you started." Everly turns on her knees and slinks along the bed, her top drooping and revealing more of her tits to my hungry eyes.

Lust consumes me.

She moves too slowly for me, so I grip her arms and lift her off the bed and help my sexy little roommate to the floor.

"That's right, Everly. Look up at me while you're on your knees. You're going to take me in your mouth and suck me so good that I forget my damn name," I say, caressing her jaw.

"Wow, Daddy. It's so big. I don't know if it's going to fit."

"You're going to make it fit. Open up and lick the tip," I command. She wraps her hand around the shaft, causing a tremor to run through me. The pleasure of her touch is about to make me come before she's even put her mouth on me. Then I feel her hot breath on the head before her sweet tongue lashes over the tip.

"Fuck." I throw my head back and groan as she slides her mouth around about the whole head, engulfing it. "That's it, girl. Take me deeper." She's doing her best to take me deeper, gagging on my cock as I stuff inch by inch into her mouth. Fuck, I'm tempted to throat fuck her, but I don't want to lose control and hurt her. I'd never forgive myself for doing anything to harm my sweet girl.

My hand wraps around the back of her head, guiding her. "Baby girl, you're going to make me come down your pretty throat."

She moans around my dick, uttering something I can't make out so I pull her off. "What did you say?"

"Please give it to me, Daddy."

"Oh I'm going to give it all to you, but that's enough." I lift her up onto her feet because I'm about to nut and I want to tear apart her pussy and finally claim her as mine.

"This needs to go." I grip the hem of her camisole and toss it on the floor. Her pert, wine-red nipples are semi-hard and pointing right at me. I run my fingers over them, stiffening them. "You came in here so I could fuck your pretty little cunt, didn't you?"

She blushes, biting down on her bottom lip.

"Answer me, or I'm going to punish you."

My hand comes down on her ass over her silky shorts. She yelps. "Yes, I did."

"Good girl. Take those off before I ruin them. Although, I'm pretty sure you've already ruined your panties, haven't you?"

"Maybe."

"Maybe? Are you lying to me?"

"No, Daddy." She pulls her shorts down, and I see she's not wearing any.

"Bad girl. Part your legs and show me Daddy's little slit." I groan, my balls aching to fill her hole. I've never wanted anything so damn bad. She's all I've ever wanted, even more than I wanted to be a doctor. The reason I had to stay away is that I didn't want to ruin my future, our future—a distraction I couldn't afford. Now that our futures are intertwined, it's time to fulfill my obsession and claim my woman.

"Your pussy is so pretty." My mouth waters at the sight. I've been thinking about her cunt for years, even when it was so damn inappropriate. "That blush is sexy. Now, keep those legs open because I'm hungry and need to eat." I lower down and kiss her inner thighs from one side to the other until I reach her slit. My tongue swipes over her pussy, licking her from the bottom up.

"Julian, oh God." I stop and look up at her, cocking my brow.

"Sorry, Daddy."

"That's right. In this room, I'm Daddy, and I'm the only one who gets this pussy."

She nods, giving me the answer I want. I return between her legs, adding a finger along with my tongue to work her into a spiral. Everly is so tight as I fuck her little hole; it drives me wild. I'm not sure how I'm going to last. Pre-cum coats the sheets beneath me.

After she comes, I can't help but watch the beauty on her face. She's the most enchanting creature I have ever seen. There is nothing I wouldn't do for this woman. Somehow I knew that a long time ago, and it's the reason I've stayed away for so long. "I love you so much, Everly. It's time that you become mine." Gripping my cock, I align it with her core. I push my way slowly into her body, inching past her entrance and hoping that I don't hurt her too badly.

Our inexperience is at a disadvantage, but there's no one else I'd rather share this moment with. "Finally," I whisper before I take her lips for a kiss.

I kiss her softness, wanting to feel every moment, letting it create a memory I will never forget. Slowly I push in deeper, going as far as I can, hoping that I'm not causing too much pain. I gently pull my hips back and then push forward again, sending myself inward and completely taking her for the first time.

She gasps as I claim her as mine. Our eyes slam shut as we each let out a hissing moan, both relief and pain taking us as her tight walls wrap around my cock. I can't even explain the bliss that fills me up.

Just as I'm thrusting deep, my phone rings until it goes to voicemail. Shit—it could be the hospital, so when it rings again, I lean over, see the phone on the nightstand, and realize it was her brother calling, not work. "It's Drake."

"Don't answer," she gasps.

A wicked, possessive thought comes over me. "Did you just tell me what to do, little girl?"

"No, Daddy."

"That's what I thought."

I smirk and slide my cock unhurriedly out and back in as I pick up the phone off the stand. Drake calls again as if it's an emergency, so I answer the phone and while fucking my woman. "What's wrong, Drake?"

"Hey, buddy. I just called to check on my sister, but she's not answering her phone."

"Yeah, I don't know what she's doing right now," I say, pressing my cock deep inside her and staying still. "Maybe she's taking a nap. I don't keep tabs on her." She smirks and then shakes her head, so I pull almost all the way out.

I fuck her wet pussy with slow, methodical thrusts. A whimper comes from her, so I lean down on my elbow and use my free hand to clamp over her mouth, keeping her quiet while I talk to her brother.

"Well, then, just let her know I called; I don't want her to think I don't care."

"You always check up on her, so I doubt she'd think that. I'll tell her you called." I end the call and set my phone on the nightstand. Smiling down at her, I add, "See what you made me do? You made me lie to my best friend."

"But you could have just not answered the phone," she sasses, squeezing her pussy around my thick shaft like her virgin body has done this a thousand times. She's a skilled temptress, seducing me.

"Damn that smart mouth of yours. I guess I didn't fuck it hard enough," I grunt.

"Maybe I just enjoyed it too much." She sticks out her tongue, but my dick is done playing with her throat for now. It's busy drilling her tight cunt, ready to breed it. She's got me fucked up in the head, and now she needs to pay for it. I know my friendship is about to be over, but all I can think about is filling her up.

"I'm sure you did. But I'm not getting out of your pussy until I nut," I tell Everly, leaning down and stuffing my fingers in her pretty mouth. "Suck." She moans around them as she does what she's told.

My hips take over, and I pump into my woman, fucking her little hole. Every muscle in my body aches as sweat builds on my skin. I hook her leg and lift it straight over my shoulder, licking her calves. "Time to come."

I'm not as gentle as I should be, but I'll make it up to her bratty ass later. "Let go," I command, and she opens her pretty mouth. "Good girl." My hand snakes down her lips to her throat where I give it a squeeze. "I love when you behave."

"Yes. Whatever you say, Daddy."

"That's my baby girl. Are you going to be a good girl and come for me?"

"Yes," she moans.

"Yes, what?"

"Yes, Daddy." Fuck, I'm not sure why I like the sound of that shit, but my dick jerks so damn hard, I'm about to come.

"Good. Give me what I want, and Daddy will give you whatever you want."

"Will you come inside me?" she asks with a soft plea.

I caress her jaw, feeling my cock swell. "Always. That's where Daddy's cum always belongs." I pinch her nipple and she cries out, pussy gripping me tight before she spasms around my meat.

"Julian, Daddy. I'm coming. Oh my God. Yes, please."

"That's it." I lean forward, moving my hands to bracket her head, gripping the bed as I pump my cock deep into her. "Fuck. You're so perfect, Everly. You get every damn drop, and you keep that shit there. You need to keep my cum inside you, little girl. Do you understand me?" I growl, not allowing her to answer before I slam my lips onto hers. I don't stop pumping until I've got nothing left and then I pretzel our legs together.

"You're mine, Everly. There's no fucking going back."

"What about my brother?"

"I don't know, but we'll have to deal with it when we get there," I whisper, dipping my head to kiss her lips, letting her feel my possession. "No one is taking you away after I've finally staked my claim, little girl."

CHAPTER EIGHT

EVERLY

OUR DOORBELL RINGS BEFORE I CAN START HIS LUNCH FOR work. Julian's in the shower, so I answer it and it's his mom. "Good morning, Dr. Holden."

"Please, call me Grace."

"Good morning, Grace. What brings you to see us?"

"I made some food and wanted to drop it off."

"Oh, okay—come on in."

"Oh, Everly, dear. I hope I haven't overstepped my place."

"Please, Mrs... Dr. Holden."

"I am Mrs. Martinez, but in the hospital, It's Dr. Holden. Still, like I said, you can call me Grace. Besides, it's not about me. I know you make Julian's food, but I thought I'd drop off his favorite."

"Everly, did you make enchiladas?" Julian asks, strolling out of the bedroom in just his boxer briefs. "Mom?" he gasps.

"Son." Her eyes widen.

"Um...I'll be right back." He dashes back into the bedroom while my cheeks burn up.

"I'll just set this here. This would explain why he was late two days ago." I clamp my lips shut, hoping the ground opens up beneath me. "Oh, sweetie, don't be embarrassed. I've been waiting for this day for so long."

"You have?" A wave of relief washes over me, but it doesn't mean that I've completely relaxed.

She presses her hand to my shoulder and gently smiles. "Yes. Julian has been a mess about you, so it's about time."

"He has?"

"I don't want to get involved, but I will say that you're a treasure to him. Still, that doesn't mean you let him walk all over you."

"Thank you." She envelops me in a hug.

I hear Julian's footsteps before I see him. "Mom, I'm surprised to see you," he pants as he enters the room barefoot in a pair of khakis and a white tee shirt with his hair a wet mess. Damn, he's so fine that I lose my breath. If his mother wasn't here, I'd run and jump on him. This is why he's always late. One of us is always coming out of the shower and looking too good to be unmounted.

"Well, I made enchiladas, and I thought I'd drop some off for you."

"You didn't have to, but I'm not going to turn them down." He rubs his flat abs, and I can't blame him because they smell fantastic. I wish I knew they were his favorite because I would have made them. Of course, I don't know how to make them, but I could have learned.

"Have you ever made them before, Everly?"

"No, I haven't."

"Well, maybe you can come to Steeleville one day and I can teach you how to make them."

"I'd like that."

"Perfect. Now, I'll leave you two alone. I have to get to the hospital for a meeting." He stares at her with suspicion.

"You knew about us, didn't you?"

"Yes, Son. I'm not a fool. You changed this past week, and let's just say you're too happy and tardy, which just isn't like you. Don't be late. I love you, but I will have to add more hours to your schedule."

"Yes, Dr. Holden," he growls.

"I love you too, Son." She kisses his cheek and then she leaves.

"She's on to us. Do you think anyone else knows about us?"

"I doubt it, but we should tell Drake soon," Julian insists.

"Yes, we should, but we both need to find the right time."
We nod, and then he kisses me fiercely.

"I'll pack up your food in your lunch bag, and then you can go."

"Promise me you'll be safe."

"I will." He kisses me and then goes back into the bedroom to finish getting dressed. My ass needs to be wearing blindfolds until he leaves for work.

With his things packed, I do my best to avoid any serious physical intimacy and head to school while Julian goes to work.

Finally, I'm almost to my class when I spot a man who appears to be watching me. He turns his head when he realizes I'm on to him. Although I should be afraid, I have a feeling this is exactly what Kate and Joey were talking about. Julian has guard dogs around me. I wave to him and then go to class.

It's been a beautiful three weeks of these warm, loving moments. I wake up with Julian's wrapped up all around my body as the sun shines through the curtains. It feels incredible, safe, and all I've dreamed of, but I have to go to class. As much as I'd love to keep it this way, we both have to get up. However, life always intrudes.

Unfortunately, it doesn't always work out the way we want. Our shifts still are the way they are. He works long hours, and I have my school schedule. My family is supposed to come and see me when I graduate with my certification, and I told Julian that's when I'd like to tell them and make it official to everyone.

He agreed, only because he doesn't want me upset before I finish school. We know Drake won't be happy about our relationship. I haven't told him that Mom was instrumental in getting us together. I feel bad about not telling him about it, but I'm afraid he'll think bad of me.

"Julian," I whisper, brushing my lips against his scruffy jaw.

"Baby, hmm. Good morning," he mumbles, snuggling even more around me.

"Good morning. It's time to get up."

"I'm so tired, and I'd rather stay wrapped up in you." He nuzzles my neck, tickling me with his beard. "You feel so good."

"So do you, but our phones have been buzzing." I moan when his fingers dip between my legs, stroking my kitty. "Jules. We need to get going." His huge cock grinds into my thigh, rubbing me in the most pleasurable ways, making me want to give in and stay in bed.

"We do, but not before I get you off," he whispers in my ear. Lazily he kisses my neck, lowering until he slides his head between my legs. I can't believe he has his face there after everything we did last night, but he can't get enough of me. His tongue and fingers don't hesitate as he devours my pussy, eating me out. My body bends to his will, creaming on his tongue with the slightest flick, and my walls clench around his fingers.

"Fuck, Julian."

"No, baby. In the bedroom, what is my name?"

"Daddy, please," I beg, my hands digging into his shoulders.

"What do you need?"

"I need to come. Please." My hips and back buck off the bed. I release my grip on him and throw my hands down on the mattress, fighting to keep my body on the bed.

"Good girl," he says, smiling over my mound. His fingers push deeper, sliding in and out of my wet pussy faster as his tongue does the same. I can't hang on much longer. Never did I expect it to be like this. His mouth continues to lick me, and I lose control.

"I'm coming," I scream, clinging to the covers. My entire body tightens and nearly convulses, and my eyes slam shut.

"Good. Come for me, Everly." He licks me up before he stands and then heads into the bedroom without another look back.

I'm so worn out that I lie there for a moment until I hear the shower. Laughing to myself, I realize he was serious about not getting up until he got me off. Checking my phone, I see a message from Drake.

I'm on my way in.

"Oh, shit." I rush to the bathroom, completely naked.

"Julian." I see him washing up, and the sight is impressive
—the way his muscles flex while doing something so basic
—but this is important.

His eyes widen as he takes in my naked state. "Yeah,
baby? Do you want to join me?"

"We can't. Drake is on his way here," I say, panic filling my
voice.

"Oh, are you serious?" He washes a little faster.

"Well, he should be in Seattle, but I'm guessing it won't be
long from his text message."

"When is he coming?" I hadn't checked that part. Silly me.
I'd been so damn frazzled by his message I hadn't
considered when he'd arrive.

"Oh, I'm panicking for nothing. It says he'll be here
tonight."

"You'll be back from class by then, and I'll be at work.
How about you climb in here and wash up with me?" he
asks, a crooked, devious smirk washing over his face.

"That's not a good idea. What if we don't tell Drake about
us just yet?" I say, trying to get out of telling Drake. As
much as I want the world to know I'm Julian's woman,
I'm terrified of my brother finding out. He might not take
it well when he finds out that we're having sex.

He goes from sensuous to frustrated. "We're not hiding our relationship." He grabs me and pulls me into his shower. The water hits my tender muscles, and it feels incredible. Julian's intense gaze is focused on me. "Listen to me, Everly Amber Mitchell. We're going to tell him the truth while he's here because I'm not going to deny the truth. You're mine." His hands skim over my shoulders, gently caressing them. "Kiss me, Everly."

I can't resist his command. My mouth lands on his with such feverish need that I forget everything else but him.

Our kisses are wet as his hands dive in my hair, roughly tugging me and then dragging me against him. He leads me backward, pinning me against the wall of the shower. He's so hungry for me, and I can't deny him. Growls and moans escape us as our wet bodies grind against each other. I love the desire so much that I crave more. It's what I'm asking for, even demanding, as I stare at him.

"I need you," I whimper between kisses, pleading for him to take me. "Please."

"I'll give you whatever you need, baby."

"I need you in my mouth," I say hungrily, wanting to give him so much pleasure like he'd just given me. I gently push him off me and lower myself to my knees in the shower stall.

A deep rumble comes from his chest as he stares at me from above. "Damn it, baby; just the idea of you taking my cock down deep in your throat is going to make me nut."

I smirk up at him, loving the power I hold over him. "I wish you would. Please, Daddy. Stuff me, fuck me, and come inside my throat."

His entire body stiffens, and his thick length jerks in his hand. "You're such a fucking bad girl. Damn, I'm in love. Open your mouth, baby."

I do, hungrily, waiting for his massive cock. I love the velvety feel of it as he pushes it past my lips and along my tongue. He stuffs his length down my throat and I take it, sucking his dick like a thick popsicle. My cheeks hollow out as my mouth tightens around him. "Fuck, you're going to make me shoot down your throat."

I suck faster and harder, but he's not having it. He quickly pulls me off him and off my feet. "No, I need to be inside you," he pants, unable to catch his breath as if he's the one who just had the nine-inch-thick bastard down his gullet.

"We need to take this to the bed, baby. There's no way I'm fucking you in the shower."

"Why not?"

"There's no room in here, and I hear it's terrible no matter how amazing the movies make it."

"I heard that too, but the bed is too far away. How about just the bathroom?" I offer.

"I like that idea." He snags two towels and wraps them around us to stop us from slipping before he carries me out of the shower. "The counter seems good enough."

I giggle as he nuzzles my neck and then licks down to my chest. "Damn, I love these sexy, plump tits." He cups one in his hand, leans down, and brings it to his mouth, sucking on it. The sensation is tender and goes straight through me. We have gotten better with every session, and he has gotten even more intense, his hands and mouth moving from one breast to the other, teasing and pleasuring me.

"It feels so good," I moan, tossing my head back, leaning on the glass mirror. "Your mouth and hands are like magic."

He kisses a path up my body, licking and sucking me until he reaches my lips, and then he whispers against them, "I need to be in your pussy right now, buried deep inside you."

"Yes, please take me."

"Fuck, I'm not going to last long."

"That's good, big boy, because we don't have a lot of time."

"You are such trouble."

"Damn right. And that's why you love me, so get over here and fuck me dirty."

"Okay, you're going to get what you asked for." He turns me around on the counter. My entire body is on the sink, knees spread wide, hands splayed above the mirror. "Keep that ass out. You want it dirty? I'm going to make you filthy."

He lines up his cock with my pussy and pushes into me from behind. "God, you're so deep."

"What did I tell you, Everly?"

"Sorry, Daddy. Messed with my head."

"You're the one who screwed with my head. Now take this dick like a good girl so we can both get out of here."

"Then fuck me good." He drills me with his hands on my hips, our still-wet flesh slapping against each other.

"Everly, you're going to make me come so fast. Fuck, you feel so good." Julian shoves it so deep from behind, fucking me raw as my breasts bounce in his hands as he cups them, squeezing them possessively.

"Damn it. I'm going to come. Holy hell."

"Fuck, Daddy, screw me so good. You're so big it hurts." Our bodies are slamming together, and the water is gone and now we're covered in sweat as the sex has steamed up the bathroom.

"And you know you love it."

"Yes, yes. I'm coming, Julian."

"Come for me, baby," he roars, pumping his load into me until we're both spent. He presses his head on my spine, and then we hear a sound coming from outside the bedroom.

"You stay in here," he warns me. He pulls out of me and then sets my feet on the floor.

CHAPTER NINE

JULIAN

SHE FOLLOWS ME OUT OF THE BATHROOM LIKE SHE DIDN'T hear me the first time. "Keep your ass in here," I growl to Everly before kissing her forehead. We hear someone outside our bedroom door. I slip on a pair of sweats and a tee shirt.

I barely open our door before Drake's closed fist lands on my face. Stumbling two steps back, I fall into the bedroom, but luckily I'm still standing. "What the fuck is wrong with you? I asked you to watch over my sister, not fuck her."

I put my palms up in an attempt to stop him from rushing me because I don't want to fight him, and I know Everly doesn't want that either. I step out of the room and close the door before he sees Everly undressed. That would set him off even more. "Calm down, Drake. It's not like that," I say as the door clicks behind me.

"Are you fucking serious right now? Because I'm pretty sure I just heard you two fucking." He presses his hands to his ears. Damn it, he still has a key. His message said he wasn't supposed to be here for hours. I'm glad the truth is out in the open, but this isn't the way I wanted it to happen. Truthfully, I wouldn't want to catch my sister having sex either.

"Considering all the years I had to put up with your shit."

"You know damn…" His fists ball up at his sides, staring at me while he chews on his bottom lip.

"Still, it's not what you think. I'm in love with Everly, and I'm going to marry her."

"The hell you are. I thought you were a good guy, but you're a scamming piece of shit. You went behind my back and tricked my sister into sleeping with you." That's the biggest bullshit I've ever heard. Well, most of it, but it still hurt that after all the years he's known me that he could believe it.

"Are you fucking serious? You threw your sister in my lap, knowing damn well she wanted to be there. I tried to deny my feelings for her because of our friendship." Maybe I shouldn't have said that because he's frothing at the mouth at that one.

"It was just a crush she was playing on years ago. It would have worn off by now, and obviously you didn't try that hard," he snarls.

"Don't talk about all the women you screw. Just because you fuck anything that walks doesn't demean our relationship. You wouldn't know what a real relationship is. I've waited for your sister all this damn time because of our friendship, letting her make her own path because I respect her."

"She's my sister, and you were supposed to be my friend. It's just wrong."

"You can be pissed all you want, but it doesn't change shit because Everly is mine and one day soon, she'll be my wife."

"Wife?" Everly gasps, coming from the bedroom fully dressed. I was so angry I don't hear her come out.

"Yes. I thought I made that pretty damn clear," I growl, sliding my hand around her waist, dragging her to my side so he can see that I'm serious.

"Drake, I'm sorry, but I'm the one who threw myself at Julian."

He wants to debate it, but he just admitted that he knew she desired me. "Mom's going to freak out."

Everly stiffens in my arms. "It's okay. We'll call and talk to her. We'll make her understand," I say.

"She's going to be furious," Drake continues.

"No, she's not. She's the one who has been telling me that Julian has feelings for me."

We both open our eyes wide at her revelation. "Mom knows?"

Everly tries to pull away from me, but I'm not having it. I tighten my grip on her because she's not getting away from me that easily. "Yes, she's the one who suggested it in the first place. Hello—it wasn't your idea or mine. She knew I was in love with Julian." I'm going to buy a nice wedding present for Carol. She deserves it.

"I'm still not comfortable with it." He ducks his head, shaking it. "I've got to go. I can't deal with this." He walks out the front door, and I let him go because Everly and I need to have a conversation, and she doesn't need his bullshit.

"What are we going to do, Julian? My brother hates us right now. Do you hate me too?" The last question startles me, and I turn her around in my arms, staring at the woman I adore with every fiber of my being. There is no motive in her eyes, no deception or even need to be reassured. What I see is pure fear.

"Hate you? For what?" I ask, needing to know what I missed.

"Because my mom and I tricked you into taking me in." Tricked? I wish I'd made her my woman sooner. All these years wasted. Technically, I knew they weren't because she had to grow up a little more and I had to get my life together, so it was right, but that didn't mean our feelings had changed, but it had been the right decision.

"Sweetheart, you didn't trick me into taking you in. If anything, it was the kick I fucking needed to get my head out of my ass. The thought of you leaving almost destroyed me in those mere seconds that your mother left me hanging before revealing that you were staying in Texas. Then they tossed out the offer of you living with me. I practically had to fight off the idea that I wasn't interested in having you sleep mere feet away from me. Temptation at my door. My desire, my hunger were just inches from me. Hating you is impossible."

I kiss her so fiercely that she can't catch her breath, and when I pull back, she presses her cheek to my chest. When I lift her face with my thumb, I can see the sadness. "Tell me what's on your mind."

"Drake hates me," she chokes out; the pain is so damn clear in her voice that it cracks my chest. I want to kick Drake's ass for hurting her. He has a lot of nerve getting pissed about us when he was screwing everything that walked.

For years, I worried that he'd be pissed because we were friends and she was young, but as he whored around, I wondered if he cared. Then he put me in the awkward position of guard duty, which only made things worse because I knew he'd hate me for it. Still, she is an adult, and so am I.

"He doesn't hate you, sweetheart; he hates me." She's fighting back tears, and I kiss the top of her head. "Don't cry. Please don't. I'll kick his ass if you cry." He deserves it. The manwhore doesn't get the right to upset her when he paraded woman after woman in here. I'm not some young punk knocking her up. I can give her everything and more.

"Please don't," she begs, clinging to my shirt. "I love the both of you, and I don't want to see you fight."

I rub her back and sigh. "This is the reason I stayed away from you. Drake's my friend, and you, little girl, are my everything."

"Gosh, this is complicated." Her shoulders slump in defeat as if she's lost something, but there is nothing that she can lose because I am her rock, her champion, and I won't let it happen.

"It really doesn't have to be, sweetheart."

She slips out of my arms, biting down on her bottom lip, hiding her eyes from me. Her voice is low as the words I don't want to hear fall from them. "Maybe we should just forget this happened."

My head shakes, and I clench my fists, irate as a motherfucker. "Are you out of your fucking mind? There's no going back, sweetheart. You're mine, and that's it. I've been holding back all this damn time, letting you tease the shit out of me with these tiny outfits, tempting me with little itty-bitty touches and taunts and then sneaking into my bedroom. Now, after taking what you've offered, you think that you can take it back? I don't fucking think so. I'll tan your fucking hide. You're mine, Everly, now and forever. End of story. Forever."

"I'm sorry, Julian. I don't know what I was even thinking." She shakes her head.

"Don't be sorry. Just don't think about that kind of stupid shit again. For the past three weeks, everything has been wonderful. Well, it would be better if I was on my physician schedule already, but when I am, we'll have more time for each other."

"Yes, we will."

"Come here." She moves into my arms. I wish I had time to ask her properly, but it will have to wait until I return from work.

"So, does this mean the guys will stop following me around everywhere?" My eyebrows shoot up, and my face heats up. "Come on. Did you think I wouldn't notice some of the prospects or even your brothers tailing me?"

"I guess they aren't hard to miss."

"Not when they're wearing their Steeleville patches and shit, or riding their bikes. I swear, anytime I saw a guy on a motorcycle, I was hoping it was you."

"I'm so sorry you were disappointed."

"Who said I was disappointed? At least I knew that meant you cared."

"I do, so damn much."

"Does this mean they're done with their job now that we're a couple officially?"

"Not a chance. They were following you around to keep you safe and to keep those frat fucks away, but nothing's changed, except everyone will know you're mine."

"I think we should call your mom, but I really have to get ready for work."

"That's a great idea. You get dressed properly, and I'll call my mom. You don't need to be on the call." I give her a kiss and hurry my ass up as she starts dialing.

"Hey, Mom. I'm just calling because I have something to tell you." She's smiling and nervous at the same time. I suppose letting your mom know you've had sex isn't easy. I'm old as fuck. Everyone in my family probably has a damn pool going around to see when I lose my damn V-card. They are a bunch of assholes.

"Is this about you and Julian?"

"Um, yeah, it is. How did you know?"

"Your brother just called me, and he was furious."

"What?"

"Yes. I tried to explain that it's fine, but he was angry about the deception. How long has it been going on?"

"A few weeks. We would have told everyone, but honestly we haven't had time to ourselves to even define this, and then we had to tell Drake first but he didn't give us a chance. He just showed up like he was trying to check up on us."

"It might be my fault."

"Why?"

"I hinted that you might be super interested in a guy, and he wasn't getting any information from Julian." She stares at me, wondering what that's all about.

"Well, it's okay. I have to get to class. Can I call you later?"

"Sure. Call me tomorrow. Harold's taking me to dinner tonight."

"Okay. I love you, Mom."

"Love you too, sweetheart."

She ended the call and sets her hands on her hips. "What do you know about this supposed guy?"

"Nothing. I didn't find out about your supposed crush. As far as I could learn, you didn't have anyone."

"So that's why you had guys following me."

"I told you I didn't want guys sniffing around you."

"You should have just asked."

"Would you have told me the truth?"

"Not entirely because that would be embarrassing, but a partial truth."

My phone goes off, alerting me that I have an hour to get to the hospital for my shift. Everly was rushing me this morning because I lost track of time since we've been together, and today is no different.

"It's time to go," she says.

"Yes, it is. When do you need to leave?"

"I've got at least another hour."

"Okay. I'm going to miss you, gorgeous." With a long, drawn-out kiss, Everly pushes me out the door, handing me my lunch so I don't forget. It's raining, so I switch to my pickup and point to the sky. "Be safe."

"Always, Doctor." She waves me off, and I head in for a long damn day without my woman.

CHAPTER TEN

EVERLY

It's been two days since Drake caught us in the bedroom. That was one sobering day. Why he'd come here on a whim to surprise us is still something I need answers for. Like, did he have suspicions? Or was he just missing us? It doesn't make sense unless he wanted to check up on me.

Either way, his anger actually helped me from being mortified about being caught. I was so worked up over his outrage that I've completely gotten over the fact that we'd been heard having sex by my own brother. I shoot him a text this morning, asking him if we can talk.

> Drake, can we have a chat?

The three dots appear, and I linger before he replies,

> Sure, I'd like to talk before I head back.

Meet me at the apartment today, please.

At twelve?

By that time, Julian will be on his way into the hospital, and my brother will be less confrontational. I quickly respond back to confirm.

Sounds good.

I'm dressed for the day and anxious, rubbing my fingers together as the clock on the wall moves closer to twelve and my Julian's still here. It's eleven forty-five, and the doorbell rings. I open it to find my brother standing there, biting down on his bottom lip, nervously rocking on his heels.

"Please come in," I say. Before Drake left that day, he'd tossed the key on the counter, not wanting to see anything again.

"Thanks." He steps in and looks around, presumably for Julian. Of course, Julian's shift actually starts an hour later than I thought, so he isn't leaving for a while longer, meaning this could get ugly.

Tension between my brother and I has never been this high. Before, I was the annoying little sister that my promiscuous brother looked after. Now, I'm the girl who ruined his friendship with his best buddy.

"Drake, Julian's getting ready for work, but you and I

need to talk." I take a seat and then pat a spot next to me, and he takes it. I love my big brother

"You're right; we need to talk." He sighs, and then he takes my hands in his, which are shaking. With all the sincerity I've ever seen, he looks me in the eye and says, "I'm sorry, Ev, but it seems that Julian's been lying to us. He's been seeing one of the nurses at the hospital."

"Oh yeah? Which one?" I need to know who she is because I refuse to believe it. We make love almost every single day, and the only reason it isn't every day is because of our schedules.

"Linda." My teeth are clenched as I hear her name. My skin crawls just thinking about this mysterious woman.

"Oh, really?" For some reason I knew he was going to say that, but it still stings because that's the number I found in his pocket—the one he tossed in the garbage.

"What makes you think he's seeing her?" I question. My stomach drops and flips while hoping that my brother is mistaken. There is no way Julian would betray me like that. He's a good man through and through. If anything, he would have just left me alone. There is no way he would mess with me, only to be cheating, especially because he's my brother's best friend.

"She told me she is pregnant with his baby." My heart stutters, even if I don't believe it. I shake my head while I listen to my brother's story. As much as I love Julian, I refuse to be a naïve girlfriend.

"You spoke to her, and she told you that she's carrying his baby?" I ask Drake.

He grows sheepish, ducking his head and running his hand through his sandy brown hair. "Well, no. I heard the nurse talking about her being pregnant with the baby of a resident, and he's one of the few residents who still works there." So, she didn't say it's Julian's, exactly, and my brother's just making an assumption because he's pissed.

"So, you don't know it's Julian's any more than you know it's yours." I toss back.

"I always use protection." The instant revulsion, knowing he screwed her too, makes me sick. I never ask Julian about his relationships because frankly I don't want to know about them. I'm young, not naïve. He's nearly thirty and gorgeous. I couldn't expect him to have remained a virgin, but that doesn't mean I have to know about any of the women. This woman is more than I want to handle.

"Protection fails," I say. As a doctor, he knows that, so his blatant denial is intentional.

I'm on my feet, clenching my fists with my chest puffed out. "I can't with this nonsense. You're only saying these things because you're pissed at Julian, and you don't want us to be together."

"I'm saying it because it's what I heard," my brother snaps, standing up and pacing. I've never seen my brother so angry.

Julian comes out from his bedroom, dressed and ready to head to work. "What did you hear?" he questions my brother, glaring at him. I hate that their friendship has been damaged by me. I want to jump between them, but I know better than to get between two big men.

With a smugness I've only seen directed at people he doesn't care for, Drake says, "I heard you're going to be a father."

Julian's eyes go directly to me and down to my belly. A smile spreads over his face. "You're pregnant, baby?"

He reaches out to cradle my waist, but then I inform him of the truth. "He's talking about Linda."

He spins around and gets in Drake's face. "I get that you're pissed that I'm with your sister, but you are going too far. You're starting some shit, Drake, but it's not going to work. I have never touched Linda." He turns to me and takes my hand, bringing it to his lips.

"I can't stand her. Just so both of you know." He gives my brother a dirty look before continuing. "I told her to back off. My mother already offered to write her up for sexual harassment, but I didn't want to create a scene. Maybe I should have taken her up on that offer."

"She's telling everyone she's pregnant with a former resident's baby," I state.

He tips his chin toward my brother with a scoff. "Then it's probably this asshole's kid, but it can't be mine because you're my one and only." The revelation comes as a shock because he'd been so sure and so intense when he made love to me.

"Are you saying…" My mind processes his words, and my heart is thumping out of my chest.

"That you're the only woman that I've had sex with." My grin is a mile wide because it's something we both shared together.

"That's why you were so uptight about women walking around naked in the apartment," Drake mutters, running his fingers through his hair.

And there goes my motherfucking grin.

My teeth slam together in anger and jealousy. I can't imagine the women touching everything with their naked bodies. "There were women walking around naked?"

"Only once, and then I demanded that it didn't happen again." I glare at my brother.

"Well, I need to head into work, so if you're going to be a prick, you can leave. You, on the other hand—I will see you later." He pulls me into his arms and kisses me hard.

The moment that Julian walks out the door, I slap my brother's arm. "Lord, Drake. What is wrong with you?"

"What? I just…"

"You could have spoken to us instead of just believing a random woman you slept with. One of the many women you banged. A man who has been your friend for nearly a decade, and you treat him like shit because he has the audacity to care for me. A man who has never lied to you. Let you stay with him and…"

"You're my sister, and he was supposed to protect you."

"I'm a woman, Drake. An adult who can make my own choices, and despite what you may think, those women you slept with were someone else's sisters and daughters too." I stand up and pace, seeing Julian's lunch on the counter. "Shit. I hate to cut this short, but I've got to go. Are you sticking around?"

"Yeah. I'll be around. I have a conference to attend, so that's really the reason I was in town." Oh. That explains why he came. It has nothing to do with us.

"I'm trying to understand this thing between you two. I really am, Everly."

"That's good, because I love him."

"He better treat you right, or I'll have to hire someone to kick his ass." I laugh as he hugs me because we both know that punch the other day did nothing to Julian. He might have stumbled, but he didn't leave a lasting mark.

We part ways, and I head down to the hospital to drop off Julian's lunch just in time to see something more than enough to rile me up. My brother may not be right, but that bitch has a serious problem and if she doesn't act right, she is going to learn quickly that I'm not as adorable as my new pink highlights make me look.

CHAPTER ELEVEN

JULIAN

I RIDE MY MOTORCYCLE INTO THE HOSPITAL FOR MY SHIFT, stopping to get gas on the way. During the entire ride, my thoughts are on the fallout between Drake and me. It's bullshit, and he's going to understand that Everly and I are together.

She's everything to me, and I knew this was going to happen between us. As I pull into a physician's parking lot, nurse Linda spots me. She stops and waits until I get off my bike, which I intentionally do at a snail's pace so that she might just keep moving along, but I have no such luck.

This damn woman doesn't understand the meaning of no. Still, just because she wants to acknowledge me doesn't mean I need to do the same. I walk straight past and into the enclosed walkway leading to the building. "Dr. Martinez, not even a good morning?"

"I'm actually busy; is there something you need?" My voice gives away my unpleasant temper.

"I'm just wondering why you haven't called me." A couple of visitors pass us, and I want to snarl because they hear her.

"There's no reason for me to call you. I'm engaged to someone else, and even if I wasn't, I'm not interested. End of story. Please don't harass me again. Do not slip your number into my jacket again, and don't flirt with me." I stop in my tracks and lean in closer to add in a hushed whisper, "And don't make up bullshit lies about being pregnant with my child."

"Oh, you heard about that," she hisses.

"Yes, I did, and I'm sure as fuck not your baby's daddy, so the fact that you put that out there should be enough to have you reported to HR. I want the rumors squashed immediately. Do I make myself clear?" I warn her, standing tall, wanting her to know I mean business. I don't realize that we have moved toward the lobby when I finally stop.

"I don't know who you think you are. Just because your mama is a fancy director doesn't mean you get to act like you're in charge. You're a resident and I have been a nurse for a very long time. You don't get to tell me what you do. I could ruin your career before it even starts. And I'll make sure your girlfriend dumps you."

"You old whore. I'm not the kind of guy who allows

anybody to take my woman away from me. Don't mess with me."

Dr. Brady approaches us. He's Head of Surgery and one of my mentors. "Oh, Dr. Martinez, there you are." I check my watch, and my shift starts in fifteen minutes, which means I would have already been in the locker room. "Oh, Nurse Saurez, I thought you were leaving."

"We were just having a private discussion." I'm seething with rage, but she smiles, gives the doctor a wink, and walks away. "See you, Julian, dear."

She saunters away, and I mutter under my breath.

I look over just in time to see that Everly is standing there with my lunch. "You forgot this."

"Remember—you're only here a little longer, and then your program is over," Dr. Brady says. I nod, and he walks away.

The tears in Everly's eyes are ready to fall and are about to destroy me. Thankfully she doesn't let them pour. Still, I can see the wheels turning in her head, and I'm not letting her get away with thinking anything dumb. Her body gives herself away. The cute little white canvas shoes squeak on the floor as she attempts to make an exit. I have my hand out before she can run, and I snag her wrist and my mouth is on hers, closing down in a deep, passionate kiss. "I love you, Everly."

"So, is that Linda?"

"Yeah, that's the fucking harpy who's spreading the lies. I just told her to back off, and she threatened me."

"She what? I should have ripped her hair out."

"No, it's okay, sweetheart. There are cameras in the garage. I think she forgot about that. I'm going to ask my mom to pull up the footage. She wants to ruin my relationship with you, but I'm not sure why."

"Because you're a hot doctor that she wants."

"It doesn't make any sense, though, because if she's knocked up, why the hell would I want to take care of her kid? She's delusional."

"Oh my gosh, Everly, you're here," my mom calls out.

"Mrs. Martinez, so good to see you." My mom wraps her in a quick hug, squeezing her hard. I'm thrilled that my family wants me with Everly because I don't need their criticism. Not that it would stop me.

"Yes, he forgot his lunch, though, so I wanted to drop it off," Everly says, blushing as she sets it down at the nurses' station.

She pats Everly's cheek. "Always taking good care of my boy. Is he taking good care of you?"

"I'm trying, Mom," I answer, sliding my hand around Everly's lower back.

"If you're not busy, I'm getting off right now. Do you want to go to Steeleville with us?"

She looks at me as if she's asking for permission. "It's up to you, sweetheart."

"I'd like that."

"Give me a kiss, and then you can head out with my mother," I demand, wanting so much more, but it's not the time nor the place.

She smiles. "So bossy."

"As long as you know what it is, then it's all good," I say, snagging her around the waist and yanking her to my chest while my other hand cradles her face. We connect in a sweet, brief kiss before someone says, "Get a room." A rumbling chuckle comes from me as Everly gasps and pulls away with embarrassment.

"Later," I grumble, and then give my mother a knowing look before adding, "Take good care of her."

"Of course, dear." She takes Everly's arm and hooks it around hers. "Let's go before he gets more distracted." I wave them off and head toward the locker rooms while she leads Everly to her office to gather her things.

***

SHE SPENT THE ENTIRE DAY AND NIGHT WITH MY MOTHER, so by the time I see my precious Everly, she's sleeping in her bed, but that's unacceptable to me. I swiftly scoop her up and carry her to my bed. "Excuse me, little girl, but where is your bed?"

"I'm pretty sure I was just sleeping in it," she mumbles sleepily, but I don't miss the attitude in her voice.

"Not your bed, but you need to be in my bed."

"Or your bed is with me."

"No, my bed is a lot bigger. Besides, I expected you to be sleeping under the covers when I got home. Why weren't you in there?"

"This." She hands me a paper.

You're my baby daddy, and will pay up. — Linda.

"The note was in the mailbox when I got home."

"Are you serious? I told you the truth when it came to my experience, Everly."

"I believe you. I'm scared, Julian. I've been in love with you since I was sixteen years old, and it took forever for you to notice me."

"I noticed you. I most certainly noticed you, Everly. Hell, the past four years were necessary so I could focus on my career and so you could grow up, or I would have done something dumb."

"Really?"

"Yes. I love you, Everly. I should have made that clear the second you walked through the door. This whole housekeeper bullshit was just to keep you inside the apartment and stop you from having to work outside. The idea of you working for another man set my teeth on edge. You belong to me."

"Do I?" she sasses.

"You know you do." My hand is on her ass, giving it a squeeze as I drag her onto my body.

"Why don't you show me?" she challenges me. All signs of sleep are completely gone from her pretty honey-colored eyes.

"You're asking for it."

"Feels like I'm always asking for it."

"Please don't stop on my account. Come on, little girl; time to beg Daddy for what you need, but there's something you need to be wearing before you do."

"What's that?"

"This." I pull the ring from my pocket and then slide it onto her finger.

"Oh my goodness, you are serious."

"I've always been serious about you, Everly. I love you." I pull off her pajama bottoms along with her panties, running my fingers over her wet pussy lips. She moans, and then I steal a kiss.

"I love you too, and I will marry you."

"I know, because there is no other option, little girl." With my cock ready, I lose all my clothes and align myself and push inside.

"You're lucky it's huge." She marvels at the ring.

Grunting, I add, "Yes, it is." I lace our fingers together and raise our hands above her head, pinning her to the mattress as I fuck my fiancée. We go at it all night long until she realizes that everything is all about her.

CHAPTER TWELVE

EVERLY

My body aches from the longest day ever. My phone rings, and my heart swells to see Julian calling. "Hey, beautiful. Are you on your way home?"

"Yes, I am. I'm surprised you're calling me."

"I had to take some time to call my lovely woman. How was your day?"

"Probably not as tough as yours, but I'm exhausted."

"I'm sorry, baby. Tell me what happened."

"We had to work on multiple clients: from kids, men, and women, and it included not just haircuts, but styling and coloring. Of course, we tag teamed some of them because hair coloring can be a full-on, all-day process for some women."

"Well, go home and get in the tub and soak, eat, and then get some good rest. When I get home, I'll wake you up with kisses and a nice massage." It sucks when our schedules are so off, but it will be nice to wake up to his touch.

"Mm…that sounds wonderful, but what about you?"

"Damn, baby girl. Don't get me started on what I want you to do to me, but none of that matters because it's all for you." Damn it. I'm no longer so tired and sore. My seat is getting hot, and I have to get some air.

"I'll see you soon. I love you."

"I love you too." I end the call and continue my drive. I'm just getting back from class for the day when I pull up to the apartment. It's a gorgeous, warm day with little to no wind, so I have the windows down. My hair is pinned up in a tight ponytail and Julian's not coming home tonight, so I don't have to worry about it looking a mess from the breeze.

My cell phone rings, and I pick it up. "Hey, Kate, how's it going?"

"I miss you, girl. You haven't been around since that day. Did your bossy guard dog punish you for getting caught by the cops?"

"Yes and no. Julian punished me in a very good way. We're together."

"What?"

"Julian and I are engaged," I squeal, bubbling with excitement. I'm so in love it's adorably pathetic.

"Are you freaking kidding me? Oh my gosh, girl. You are so freaking lucky. That man is so damn fine, and I knew he was keeping tabs on you for a reason."

"I guess so. He wanted to protect me while he was at work." I noticed my guards and even said hello to them when I visited Steeleville with his mom. They nearly paled when they saw me, as if they were going to get Julian in trouble.

"Yeah, and keep all the college guys away too." I would be offended by that, but my man is faithful to me, so it's only fair that he is trying to level the playing field. The damn man is obsessed.

I put up the windows, turn off the engine, and then hop out of the car.

"What the fuck?" I'm about to knock this bitch out. I can't believe she showed up here after everything she's done. "Hey, Kate, I got to let you go. I got this bitch that doesn't know what the fuck no means."

"Do you need help?"

"Nope, Julian's guard dogs are lurking," I remind her. I end the call and stand right in front of Linda, who is about ten feet away from our apartment door. "Do you have a motherfucking problem?"

"Who are you?" Linda asks.

"I'm Julian's fiancée. Who the hell are you?" I question, already knowing the answer but wanting to hear it from her mouth.

"I'm the mother of his child."

A laugh of disbelief falls from me. "Oh, please—spare me. I already know you didn't sleep with Julian." I'm about to walk away when my brother Drake hops out of his rental.

"Linda, why are you harassing my sister?" Drake barks out, storming toward us.

She squints her eyes at my brother. "You look familiar."

"You don't remember who you fucked?" I bark out in contempt.

"What? You and I never..." She shakes her head in disgust as if my brother's ugly, which he's not. If anything, he's hot—not to me, of course, but girls love him and that's why he has so many flings.

He crosses his arms and nods. "Yes we sure the fuck did, and Julian ran into you in the kitchen that morning but then went to work."

She continues to shake her head in confusion. "Wait...that doesn't make any sense. I don't remember you, but I remember him." There's a pity I actually feel for this woman as a sick realization hits me. Her mind has events twisted, and I'm not sure if it's because of alcohol or something else, but I trust my man and my brother.

"You think you fucked him here?" Drake asks, sounding concerned, pointing to the apartment.

"Yes, I remember going out, and then my memory is fuzzy. I had great sex, but it was dark and then he offered me some coffee the next morning before leaving for work."

"He might have offered you coffee, but you were in bed with me that night. Julian was my roommate. He was pissed about all the women coming and going, but he's still a gentleman and civil. And most certainly, he doesn't bring women home."

She presses her hand to her head, tears welling up in her eyes. "How could I not remember anything?"

"How smashed were you?"

"I was pretty drunk. It was a bad couple of days for me." She bites down on her bottom lip, and I wonder if there's a story behind it, but it's not my problem as long as she stops harassing Julian.

"We were both pretty wasted, but I'm sure I used protection that night."

"I'm confused. I need to go." She gets in her car and drives off. Damn, she shouldn't drive off like that when she's that emotional.

I grab my brother's bicep and say, "I think you need to talk to her. If she's pregnant with your baby…"

He presses his hand to his forehead, looking at her fleeing vehicle and then back at me. "I know. Fuck. I swear Linda was all over me and we had a great time. How did she not remember me and think she screwed Julian?" My brother looks truly defeated. Does he actually like her, or is he feeling something closer to a blow to his ego?

"Like she said, she remembered the lights were off. Do you remember all the faces of all the women you sleep with?" I remind him.

"Fuck..." Drake runs his fingers through his dark, fluffy brown hair. "I'm sorry for all of this, Ev. I need to know something."

"Okay."

"Are you and Julian serious?"

"Yes. He asked me to marry him." I show him my hand.

"Wow, Julian wasn't playing. I wish I wasn't such an asshole about the two of you."

"Well, you can make it up to him later, but I think you should figure this thing out with Linda. If she is having your baby, then you have bigger issues on your plate."

"You're telling me. Look, I've got to go. Can I call you later?"

"Sure." He gives me a hug and then leaves. I feel better about the whole thing with Julian, but I'm so worried about my brother, whose problems got a lot worse. Could I be an aunt some time in the near future?

"DRAKE, WHAT BRINGS YOU OVER HERE TO SEE US?" I ASK AS Drake enters our apartment. I'm surprised he was able to extend his stay for an extra couple of days.

He "First, I came over here to apologize. As much as it disturbs me to see you two together, Julian is a great guy, even if you guys are into some kinky shit."

I roll my eyes. "Thank you. That's big of you. Even if it's coming from a super player who sleeps with anything that breathes."

"Not anymore." He throws his hands up. "No way in hell. I just had myself tested. Second, I'm getting the safety put on my gun. From now on, only shooting blanks. Then I'm taking it easy with the ladies because there is no damn way am I getting mixed up with the trouble with Linda."

"So what happened?" Julian asks, sitting me on his lap, and Drake, to his own credit, doesn't flinch.

"Well, first, she actually went to a doctor and had more tests done, like a full ultrasound and bloodwork. She's much farther along than initially expected. It would have been weeks before we hooked up. It was her boyfriend's baby. The night we hooked up was before I finished my residency, so the kiddo isn't mine. And apparently, I wasn't the guy she wanted to sleep with. The reason she remembered you so damn much was because her drunk ass that night had really wanted to sleep with you."

"Sorry," Julian remarks drolly, shrugging while sliding his hand slowly up my shirt and rubbing my belly.

"It's fine. Frankly, sex gets boring when you get so damn drunk. It blurs into the next one. I needed a reason to slow down."

"I can't believe it," I mutter.

He chuckles. "I didn't say I'd stop. Just take a breather."

"That's good news."

"So what are you two love birds up to?" he questions.

"We were about to watch a movie and have dinner."

"That's good. I came to say goodbye. I have to fly back to Seattle tonight. Hopefully next time we will have some fun." I hope so because I don't like the awkwardness between them. I love them both and want them to get along like they always did. Especially because we're in this for the long haul.

"We will." We give each other hugs, and Julian walks my brother to his rental. They share a brief conversation and one more hug before my brother gets in his car and drives off.

CHAPTER THIRTEEN

JULIAN

WE'RE SUPPOSED TO BE LEAVING FOR THE BIG CELEBRATION IN Steeleville today. Everly graduated with her certification, but my little temptress stepped out of the bedroom in the tightest black dress that sent me to my knees. "You are perfection, and all mine."

"How do you like it?"

"It's a masterpiece, but it would look better on the floor," I recommend, sliding my hands onto her hips.

"We're going to be late."

"Whose fault is that?"

"I don't know what you're talking about." Her feigned innocence is adorable until my left hand slides down her ass and under her dress to find no panties when I caress her soaking wet slit.

"That's it. Bend over, baby. Show Daddy what you got for me. You think you can sneak out of this apartment without any panties on and there won't be any consequences? Think again, beautiful." She leans forward, hands on the edge of the bed. I pull her dress up to her waist and then rub both cheeks with the appreciation they deserve.

When she moans her satisfaction, I pop her ass cheek and then stuff my fingers into her hole, drenching them and watching the way she mewls, tossing her head back.

"So damn bad. Get on the bed on all fours." Everly climbs up on the bed, spreading her legs with her pussy on display from behind so I can see everything. With hands pressed on the mattress, I can see her ring, and I love the way it shines.

And my mouth waters like a damn leaking faucet. I'm salivating at the sight, and so is her glistening cunt.

"Fuck," I groan, stroking my cock. It's such a delicious view. Everly's body looks ripe for the taking. She looks sexy with her ass up, giving me a perfect view.

She turns her head, hair flipping over her shoulder. "Is that what you want? Do you like what you see?"

"You know I do."

Her perfectly sculpted brow arches with sass. "Then what are you waiting for?"

"Are you telling me what to do?"

"You know I'm the one in charge."

"We'll see about that, little girl." A tiny shiver passes over her body as she waits for me. I kneel on the bed, moving behind her and into position, allowing my hand to travel over her thighs and then over her ass. Damn, I'll never get enough of this round, juicy ass.

It's fantastic to caress her round cheeks and then give her a good smack on that luscious bottom. She yelps so loudly that my dick hardens even more. I stare into her eyes and ask, "Who's in charge?"

"I am."

"Ah, you are testing me, little brat?" I growl, teeth clenching. With my hand flattened, I repeat on the other cheek, watching her bottom turn pink. Everly yelps, looking back at me with a pout and then narrows her gaze, filling it with defiance.

I repeat my question. "Who's in charge?"

"Me," she answers; this time her voice is a little softer. I fist her hair and pull her head back a little, leaning in and whispering, "I'm sorry—I didn't hear you correctly. What was that, baby?"

"I said 'me.' I'm in charge."

"I think you like Daddy spanking you."

"I don't know what you're talking about." The blush and smile on her face is a dead giveaway, but I let her play her games because I love it as much as she does.

"I'm just going to have to find out for myself." My hand slides over her ass, which she eagerly pushes into my hand. I move down her cheeks right between her divide, gliding over her slit and dipping my fingers into her slick center, and my girl is soaked.

A soft whimper falls from her lying lips.

"Yep, you're a little liar. You're drenched, honey—soaked to the core."

"I don't know what you mean," she protests.

"Keep lying to me, and I'm not going to let you come."

She gasps. "You wouldn't dare."

"Try me."

"You're not a nice daddy."

"And you're a little brat."

"I promise to be a good girl."

"But will you be?" I question, staring into her gorgeous, pleading eyes while knowing I'd never hold back from her. There is nothing I won't give this woman. I love Everly, and everything I did was for her—even this.

"I will; I promise." She rubs her ass up and down, sending her cunt over my fingers, letting them go deeper into her wet slit. "Please, Daddy."

I thumb her clit. "You know I can't deny you anything. Be a good girl and come over here and apologize properly, and then I'll give you what you want." She moves, pulling free from my fingers and I'm almost upset, but then her pouty lips wrap around my stiff length, and I'm no longer frustrated. "Fuck."

"Everly, you undo me. You keep that up, and I'm going to come down that pretty little throat." She sucks harder. I fist her hair and pull her off my dick. She looks so fucking perfect with her puffy, swollen lips and red lipstick smeared with a bit of dribble still attached to my cock that she wipes away. "I thought you said you were going to be a good girl."

"Looks like you don't want to come."

"I want to come in your pussy, baby. I want you to walk into that party with my cum dripping down your thighs, letting everyone in the place know that you're mine." Her thighs clench together.

I bend her over the bed and stuff her from behind, filling her up with one long, singular thrust, bottoming out in her narrow pussy. She squeezes me so tight that I swear she's going to break me, but I stay still and my needy Everly begins to move, bouncing her ass back on my cock and fucking herself on me. I lean forward, my fingers wrapping around her shoulders and holding on as I look down between us, seeing my cock disappear inside her warmth.

The rush of desire overrules me as I pull out, so I pick her up and place her further up on the bed. "I want you to ride me. Fuck yourself on my cock." When I sit down, I set her legs on the outside of mine, and then I lift her onto my painfully hard pole.

"Oh my. Oh…" A moan falls from her lips, parting as she tosses her head back, hands clinging to my biceps so she doesn't slip back.

"Good girl. I'm so glad you can take me all the way down."

"It's so big, but feels so right." She gently lifts up and then down, taking it gingerly as she adjusts to the position, riding me so nicely. "Oh, Jules. You are so deep inside me. Do you think it makes a difference when it comes to the baby?"

"Baby?"

"Um…yes."

"Fuck," I groan, flipping her onto her back and pumping faster as my mouth takes hers in a rough, possessive kiss. "You're mine, and you're having my baby." I lose my damn mind, and I start shooting my load before I can think. I want her to come with me, and I don't have to worry because her walls flex around my cock.

"Yes, Daddy."

"That's right. I'm your daddy." I kiss her gently and then pull out and slide down to her belly. Softly placing a kiss there, I whisper, "I'm your daddy, too."

An hour later, we make it to Steeleville where every Steele Rider and Everly's family have gathered to celebrate her graduation. I didn't expect the party to be as badass as it is, but my mother doesn't hold back.

"Congratulations, Everly," Mrs. Steele says.

"Thank you."

"So the salon is anxiously waiting for you to come over and start working when you have time."

"How about she starts off slow?" my mother says.

"Why?" I ask.

"Because you won't see each other if she's always in Steeleville and you're at the hospital and coming home at odd hours. You two barely saw each other before, and you lived in the same apartment. Everly didn't have to work all day outside the house."

"Are you trying to stress me out?"

"No, I'm just trying to prevent fights now."

"Your mom is right. Your residency doesn't end for another eight months, so maybe we can talk about a two-day schedule until I can work something out. Would that work for the salon?"

"Of course. We'd love to have you there as much as we can," Mrs. Steele adds.

"I want you to be happy," I tell Everly.

She huffs, giving me an expectant look as if I'm missing something. When I stand there without a response, she leans in and whispers through clenched teeth, giving me a scowl. "Soon, I'll need time off."

"Fine. Of course. If that's what you want, baby girl. I'm good with it. All I care about is pleasing you. Now, can we talk about our wedding?"

"Oh my goodness. Wedding?" Everly's mother cheers, coming over to our side. "When are we doing this?" she asks, rubbing her hands together, causing the bangles on her wrists to jangle. I like my future mother-in-law a lot. Carol is a nice woman with a heart of gold who loves her daughter and respects me.

"I want to marry Everly as soon as possible, but it's up to her."

"Can we make it simple so that we can have it pretty fast?"

"Well, this party took me a week between my meetings. If you want, I can take a month to plan it, and then you will have a spectacular bash."

"Yes," my sister Isabella says, coming over and hugging Everly. "I don't know what you're talking about, but a party sounds great."

"Everly and Julian's wedding."

"Even better. I've been waiting for them to tie the knot already. Julian took forever to even ask her to be his girl."

"Relax. We're already having a baby," I blurt out. My hand slams on my mouth, and Everly's eyes widen as her mouth pops open. I take her hands in mine. "I'm so sorry."

"It's okay. I guess we were going to tell them soon." She turns to my mother and hers and says, "I don't know how far along I am, but yes, we're having a baby." The ladies all cheer, drawing attention from everyone around.

"I guess the cat's out of the bag."

"We have a lot to celebrate. A round of champagne and a glass of juice for me please," Everly says. I squeeze her to my side and kiss her lips.

"I love you. Thank you for not giving up on us."

EPILOGUE

JULIAN

I watch her from the window as she finishes a client's hair, and I can't take my eyes off the way she moves: the subtle sway of her hips to the flow of her hair from the fan's breeze. She laughs at a joke about something the owner says, and my heart nearly explodes.

My dick stiffens as she presses her hand to the small swell of her belly, knowing my baby is growing inside. We don't know if we're having a boy or girl just yet, and I can wait because I've learned patience, but my Everly is all full of chaotic energy. I had to eat her twice and then fuck her into a deep sleep so she would rest. We have an appointment in twenty minutes.

It's now that her coworker spots me staring, and she smiles. She taps Everly's shoulder and says something. Then my gorgeous wife turns around, and the wide grin on her beautiful face turns me into an animal. I want to burst through the glass just to get to my wife. It's stupid and wild, but my entire body lights with violent, feral energy. She grabs her purse and waves them off.

When she reaches me outside, my wife scowls. "Stop that. Those women don't need to see my sexy husband in his predator state. You're about to attack, Hubby."

"I don't know what you mean," I growl, my words almost unintelligible.

"Julian. I don't know what has come over you, but you're positively feral. Still, it will have to wait until we see the doctor. I can't have cum dripping down my legs when they examine me." Hearing her say cum only makes me want to fuck her more.

"Damn it, woman. You are driving me insane."

"I thought I was the horny one," she teases, putting her hand in mine.

"Come on. It's only a short walk to the office and even though it's nice out, I'm starting to get a chill."

"You're cold, baby? We'll take the truck." I turn her around and head to my pickup truck that's parked down the block from her shop.

She lets go, stopping dead in her tracks. "By the time we park and walk inside, we'll have walked the same distance." She rolls her eyes and takes my hand again.

I take off my light quarter zip sweater since I'm wearing a button-down shirt underneath. "Put this on."

"What about you?"

"I'm not cold. Don't argue with me, little girl."

"I'm not a little girl. I'm a married woman." That sass always gets me hard because I know damn well she wants to play.

"You'll always be Daddy's little girl," I growl in her ear.

"Fuck, Jules. That's not fair. I hope I don't need any female exam today because I'm going to punish you."

"I deliver the punishment, baby. It's been a while since I've turned those cheeks bright pink, so keep talking back."

"Whatever, Dr. Martinez. I don't take orders from you, so you keep this." She shoves the sweater into my chest, but that's not going to work. I grab her around the waist and slide my hands around her body before dragging her between two buildings.

"Mrs. Martinez, I find your behavior quite unacceptable, and I'm so tempted to punish you right before your appointment," I grunt, rubbing my hips into hers, grateful her swell is so small at this moment.

"Maybe we should reschedule."

"You are a silly little thing. I promised to give you what you wanted, so we will go in now and then I'm going to take you home and punish you really good. You're going to be begging for my dick before the night is over, and then you'll remember to listen to me. Now, give me a kiss so we can go inside."

She lifts onto her toes as I lower my head, snatching her mouth in a deep kiss. We make out for a minute when the alarm on my phone goes off. It's a reminder for the appointment.

She pulls away. "Please don't tell me you have to go in."

I shake my head and then kiss her forehead. "No, that's just telling us to move our ass or we will be late."

A minute later, we're in the lobby of the doctor's office and my wife is swimming in my sweater, looking absolutely adorable and messy. Her hair and lips are chaotic, but the smile gives it all away.

"Everly, Julian, this way."

"Come on, beautiful. Let's see who we created." I tap her ass, and I don't miss the smirks on the faces of a couple of nosy neighbors. I love Steeleville, and I'm sure everyone will be gossiping about it later. No fucks given. Loving Everly has been the smartest thing I've ever done. I wish I'd done it sooner.

Six hours later, I hold my completely sated and sleepy wife in my arms as we stare at our little baby boy in his first picture. "Wow, your parents are going to lose it."

"They sure are."

"So is your mom."

"Do you think Drake would like to be his godfather?"

We laugh hysterically because Drake doesn't want any responsibility. After getting the scare of a lifetime with

Saurez, he doesn't want to be anywhere near children. "How about we find someone who is a bit more kid friendly?"

"You have so many people."

"And we have time. Are you hungry or sleepy?"

A yawn escapes her gorgeous lips. "I have my answer. Sleep, and we'll eat in the morning before I head to the hospital."

"You make the perfect Daddy."

"You'll always be my special girl." I kiss her and let her rest while I look at my son again. This is what I've waited for all my life. My heart swells with anticipation. Everly is everything to me, and it all started with a glance from a hundred feet away. I fell in love with my best friend's little sister, and I tried to stay away, but it was futile because she was always meant to be mine.

EPILOGUE

EVERLY

"Happy anniversary, beautiful," he says, entering our bedroom with a pair of jeans and black boots tucked under them. His black tee fitted to his perfectly sculpted chest elicits all kinds of filthy thoughts from me. Nothing has changed in nearly a decade and a half since I first saw him.

"Why, don't you look handsome. Where are we going?" I ask. It's our fifth wedding anniversary, and he's been planning a date for us.

"Well, that is a surprise. Get your pretty self over here and let's go."

"Where are you taking me? You know I don't like surprises."

Julian spits out a chuckle, spanking me on the bottom. "Yes, you do; stop lying. Always such a brat," he mutters, shaking his head at me as he pulls me close.

"Yes, I am, Dr. Martinez." I press my hand on his chest, loving the feel of his heart beating strongly under my palm.

He presses his hand against my cheek, staring into my eyes with the love I witness every day. "I can't believe it's been five years already."

My grin spreads across my face until my lips brush against his palm, turning slightly to give it a kiss. "I know, right? So much has happened in that short time."

He squeezes me tightly and then leans back with me in his arms to say, "Yes, you've given me two sons and are nearly the lead stylist."

"And you're the head physician in the ER."

"One of the head physicians. You forget Steeleville has created a lot of amazing doctors over the years." He's correct; Steeleville and the Riders themselves have raised doctors and nurses over the years, creating a talented bunch who give back to the community. I'm extremely proud of my husband.

"It's a hot day. Are we riding or driving?"

"Riding, in more ways than one," he growls, nuzzling his nose along my jaw and sliding it down my throat.

"I should change." Before we were together, he hated my outfits because he was so possessive of me. He still is, but now I'm his and there isn't a soul that could make me leave him. I love this man, so he loves to see me in shorts and a tight top.

"No, baby. You're perfect like that," he insists, slipping his hands possessively over my hips.

"Thank you. Are Ricky and Julian having fun?"

"Yes, but I think my parents are the ones having too much fun with all their grandbabies."

"They have seven so far," I comment. Every time I turn around, one of us pops out a baby. Julian and I took a break from having babies, but since we started trying again, we haven't been so lucky—until now. I haven't told my husband yet. It's one of my anniversary surprises.

"Give me your hand, Mrs. Martinez."

"I already did."

"Forever," he answers, snatching my hand and lacing our fingers together and bringing it to his lips. "Let's go." We climb onto his bike, and he hits the ignition while I wrap my arms around his strong waist.

"Put on your helmet." I do, and it goes dark.

"What the hell?"

"It's part of the surprise, Wife."

"Okay."

"Trust me. It's worth it," Julian promises, voice husky with lusty desire. My body melts against him.

Ever since my first ride, I've never let go. Being on the bike with my husband feels like flying, and I can't get enough.

Other than family, no other woman has been on his bike, and that has been intentional. Only me.

The ride seems to be a long one, and then we come to a stop and he turns off the engine. "Don't take it off just yet, baby girl. When your phone rings, take off the helmet."

"Okay." A minute passes, and then it goes off. I take the helmet off my head, and I'm in the middle of a field that's familiar. There is a row of empty seats, and up ahead is a dais where my husband stands, a mic prepared. Instead of a banner commemorating the graduating class, it reads *Happy Anniversary, Mrs. Everly Martinez!*

Many years ago, I stood here and gave a speech about how grateful I was to be given a chance to even be born. How doctors were a huge part of my life. And now I stand here to say how grateful I am to be the husband to a woman who sat right there all those years ago unaware of what she'd done to me. She stole my heart—captivated my soul when I couldn't even approach her. I waited, hoped, dreamed that one day the time would be right. She took control and demanded that I claim what I wanted. I did. Now, I'll never go back to a life without her. She's perfect in every single way, from the smile she gives me when she wakes up, the frown when the kids drive her insane, and to the screams when I'm bringing her to ecstasy. Her happiness, her pain, her sadness are all mine, and I live for her. Everly Amber Martinez, you are my everything. I love you. Happy Anniversary.

Tears fall from my eyes as I stare at the only man I've ever loved. I stand up as he storms down the path. When he reaches me, he growls, "What I wanted to do the first time." His mouth slams on mine as he wraps me up in his arms.

"I loved you then, and I'll love you forever, Dr. Martinez." I wrap my legs around his waist, and we fall to the grass. I land on his chest with my knees hitting the ground below. Giggling, I kiss my husband's face.

"Are you okay, my beloved wife?"

"Never better. I'm glad we didn't act on our feelings then."

"Although I'm sad I waited so long to take what was mine."

"True, but at least I got to finish my certification before our son came."

"Yes. Julian came quickly, and Ricky wasn't far behind. You didn't have a lot of time to focus on your career."

"It's okay. I've been so happy to have your babies."

"I love seeing you rounded with my babies."

"Do you?"

"Yes."

"That's good, because you're going to see it again."

"Yes?"

"I'm pregnant," I say, waiting for my handsome husband's reaction. He lifts us into a sitting position and turns me so

I'm sitting across his lap. His arms wrap around me and my shoulder brushes against his chest.

"Are you sure you're okay?"

"Never better," I whisper, brushing my lips against his.

"Careful, baby girl."

"I haven't been your baby girl in years. I'm an old woman now."

"Wife, you'll always be my baby girl. Now, let's get out of here before we get caught doing something indecent."

"You want to do something indecent to a pregnant woman?"

"Not a pregnant woman. I want to violate my pregnant wife until she's screaming my name while coming all over my face, my hands, and my cock."

"Then we better find somewhere to go because I'm holding you to that."

"Now onto the next part of the evening, Mrs. Martinez." The wicked grin that spreads across his face thrills me in so many ways. I'll be forever grateful that I convinced my family to let me move in with him.

"Onto the rest of our lives," I add, smiling as he carries me to his waiting motorcycle.

THE END

ALSO BY C.M. STEELE

A Best Friends Duet:

Picture Perfect * Instant Obsession

Best Friends Series:

Always You * His Dirty Secret * Sleep Tight

Bianchi Crime Family:

Married to the Mob * Captured by the Mob * Owned by the Mob

Cavanaugh Security Series:

Protecting Macy * Securing Blake

The Cline Brothers of Colorado:

Whatever it Takes * Taking Whatever He Wants * Finding
Paradise

The Conti Crime Family Series:

Alessio * Dario * Enrico * Matteo * Gio

Dirty Boss Series:

My Pet * My Cookie * My Flower * My Valentine

(Now on Audio)

The Falling Hard & Fast Series:

Falling for the Boss * Falling for the Enemy * Falling Hard

The Fiore Family:

Christmas with the Beast * Christmas with the Boss * Christmas
with the Sheriff

Gimme Series:

Sugar * Luck * Rain * Cream * Heat * Love

Holly Hills Christmas:

Holiday's Cookies * Celeste's Secret * Bethany's Crush

(Now on Audio)

The James Family:

No Choice * No Way Out * No More Waiting

Keepsakes:

Keeping Blossom * Keep in Mind

The Lamian Wars:

Bound * Reveal * Release

All Hallows Eve

The Middleton Hotels:

Built for Me * Built to Last * Built Strong

Built Over Time * Built Overnight

Nothing but Trouble Series:

Taking the Bait * Taking the Mafia Princess

The O'Connell Family:

Claiming Red * Burning for Claire

Claiming Abby * Reminding Red

Obsessed Alpha Series:

Stone * Cole * Graham

Theo * Maddox * Alessandro

Tony * Cormack * Cameron * Jake * Sawyer

Reynolds Ranch Series:

Lara * Tobias

A Rocky Start Series:

Rocky Waters * Her Rock * Rocky Start

A Rough Hands Novella:

My Miracle * Nailing my Wife

Say Something Series:

Say Uncle * Say Please * Say Uncle: Doggy Style

Second Generation:

Say Yes

Seasons of Love:

Wet Summer * Autumn Falls * Winter Frost

Sister Switch:

Testing Her Professor * Assisting Her Boss

A Steele Christmas:

Mason's Winter * Perfectly Wrapped * The Company You Keep

A Steele Fairy Tale:

My Gold * My Forever * My Property * My Prince Charming

A Steele Riders Family Novella Series:

Sammie * Roxie * Mike * Dylan

Steele Riders MC Series:

Boomer * Mick * Jackson * Doc * Beast * Ghost

Wrench * Blade * Boss * Cowboy * Law *Cyber

Steele Riders MC 2nd Generation Series:

Will * Julian * Simon * Miles

Southern Hospitality:

Down South * Gone South

Sweet Temptation Bay:

A Taste Of Honey * The Mayor's Surrender * Trapped with my Stalker

Sweetheart's Treats:

Sweet Surprise * Doctor's Orders, Sweetheart * Sweet Surrender

Twin Sin:

Stalk Me Please * Sinful Intent

White Wolf Ridge Series:

Turner

Wolfe Creek Series:

Wolfe's Den * Beta: Her Alpha

Raging Kane * Written in History

Standalones:

Auctioned to the Kingpin* Buying Love * Christmas Compromise
* Conquering Alexandria

Ecstasy Captured * Grant's Deal * In Heat * Intense

Killer Abs * Love Discovered * Loving My Neighbor *
Lucky Ride

Mrs. Valentine * My Christmas Gift

Rainy Days * Stormy Nights * Red Hot Nights

Room Service * Scarred * Sharp Curves

So Wrong * Standing There

The Mobster's Virgin * The Wedding Guest * Unexpected

www.ingramcontent.com/pod-product-compliance
Lightning Source LLC
Chambersburg PA
CBHW021015180626
46814CB00003B/1289